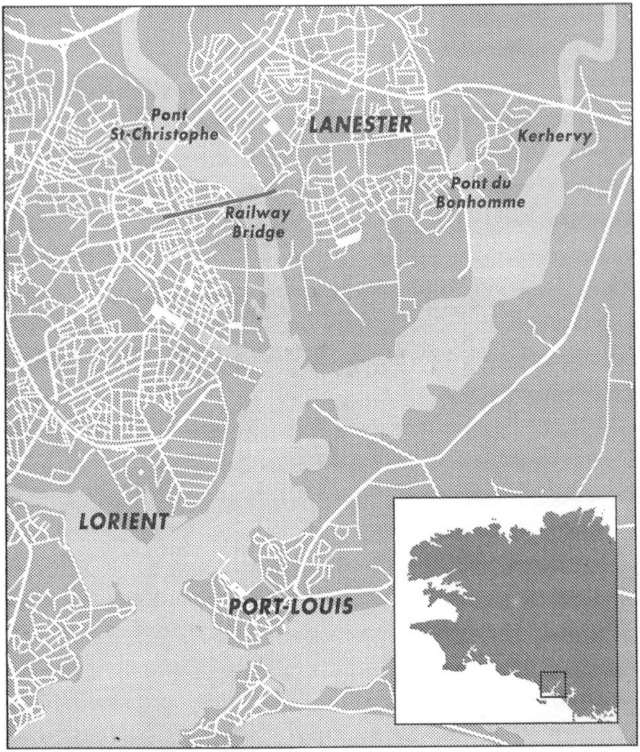
Pont
St-Christophe
LANESTER
Kerhervy
Pont du
Bonhomme
Railway
Bridge
LORIENT
PORT-LOUIS

Drizzly days in Lanester

Jean FAILLER

Drizzly days in Lanester

ÉDITIONS DU PALÉMON
ZA de Troyalac'h - N° 10 - Rue André Michelin - 29170 St-Évarzec

With thanks to:

Pierre DELIGNY
Nicole GAUMÉ
- JF -

Linda LEE
David PEARCE
Danièle LARUELLE
- AP -

First published in 1998 by
Éditions du Palémon
ZA de Troyalac'h
10, rue André Michelin
29170 St-Evarzec
FRANCE

Originally published in French as *Les bruines de Lanester*
by Éditions du Palémon, St-Evarzec.

ISBN 978-2-907572-84-2

CHAPTER I

The body of Maurice Toussaint, also known as *Mo* or *Winklestar*, depending on the degree of intimacy one might have had with the deceased, was found at low tide by Aimable Maugracieux, master gunner, presently retired.

If it hadn't been for the strap of his carpet-bag, Mo, now spread-eagled on the black muddy bed of the river Scorff, right in the middle of the East India Company's log dock, would long have drifted out with the ebb tide. However, the strap had got caught around one of the old worm-eaten stakes that used to hold in the ship builders' lumber, left there to soak, tide-in, tide-out, for several months. This practice aimed to prepare these landlubbers to their future element, the sea, where, once assembled by virtue of Man's genius, the keels, ribs, timber heads, planking and one thousand other pieces cut up by the carpenters of the nearby Arsenal would become warships.

For his last voyage, Mo had moored himself to these stakes, initially designed to hold other trunks than human.

Aimable Maugracieux stops, freezes, and swears in front of his macabre discovery.

'Bloody hell!'

He approaches the deceased gingerly, as if fearing some dirty trick.

When alive, Winklestar had been quite harmless. This gentle vagabond's ambition had been restricted to two very definite objectives: finding something to drink when he woke up, and sleeping when he had drunk.

This time, he had certainly drunk, like a fish you could say, except that the beverage had been most unusual for him: water! A substance quite foreign to Mo, whether for internal or external use. Moreover, this was salt water. At last a liquid that wouldn't give him a hangover as, you'll agree, hangovers usually hit you when you wake up and that's something poor Mo certainly isn't going to do for a long time.

Totally harmless when alive, Winklestar doesn't look very fearsome now he's dead. But... you never know. Aimable Maugracieux' snub nosed face suddenly crinkles with annoyance. He's going to have to report this to the police, and that means hassle: questions, statements, in other words, a considerable waste of time. Nothing good is going come out of all this.

On top of that he'd planned to pick some winkles for his supper, definitely not on schedule any more. And will Aimable Maugracieux ever be able to enjoy his winkles any more? Not so sure. The few fair sized specimen presently exploring the body's hollowed orbits aren't exactly appetizing.

Ironically, winkle picking had been Mo's main trade, hence his nickname. With an expertise borne from long practice, he'd tracked them down beneath the kelp growing in the mud flat. When his plastic bucket was full, sometimes earlier when thirst or hunger took priority, he sold them in Lorient or went to the local fishmonger's and traded them against a litre of red wine, his only currency where bartering was concerned.

He would then take the metal gangway of the railway bridge over the Scorff which stood fifteen metres high, an uncomfortable height when the wind was growling through the structure's metal crosspieces and the Paris-Quimper train was crawling noisily over it.

Mo wasn't the only one to use this shortcut. Quite a few people from Lanester do so regularly, overcoming ugliness, windiness and giddiness all the more easily that it spares them the 2 kilometre detour upstream to the Pont Saint-Christophe[Tr. Note].

Yes, Maurice Toussaint made a living off the winkles and now the winkles are living off him. Mother Nature's implacable law: eat or be eaten…

A few green crabs scuttle away on hearing the loud sucking noise Aimable Maugracieux' boots make as he ploughs through the sticky mud. Two fat herring gulls perched on a neighbouring stake and casting longing glances at the body fly away heavily, protesting with loud raucous cries. They land a few metres away, never letting their cold beady eyes off this great lump of meat that Mother Sea, in her infinite goodness of heart, has thoughtfully provided.

Tr. Note : *"Pont" means bridge. The Pont Saint Christophe crosses the river Scorff between the large seaport Lorient and its suburb, Lanester.*

He's dead, perceptively notes Aimable Maugracieux. What does he think, this master gunner? That Winklestar is there for the fun of it?

Aimable stays there a while, pondering on what he should do, arms hanging, undecidedly balancing from one foot to the other, the mud gurgling away with each change of footing. At last, having more or less established that this here individual doesn't require urgent care, he tramps off to warn the authorities.

Maugracieux phones the cops from a telephone booth standing by the dockside and it costs him one franc fifty. A franc fifty at his expense, of course. At least the booth isn't out of order, thank God for small mercies! They often are nowadays, and sometimes they don't put your call through but won't give you your money back either. It had already happened to Aimable Maugracieux. He'd even been all the way to the central post office to complain. But do you think he got a refund? No way!

'For one franc' had sneered the postwoman. Aimable would have quite happily slapped the cheeky old cow. The other idiots in the queue had stood up for the old bag as well: 'A franc! Does one waste a hard-working civil servant's precious time for one franc!'

So he'd given up and left, grumbling to himself. A franc is a franc thought Aimable. On top of that, it was a matter of principle, which made this franc doubly symbolic. But principles have gone to pot in this country; that's why France is in such a sorry state these days. Oh, how he would have loved to hold these protesters under his thumb when he was deputy instructor in the barracks of Hourtin. By God! He would have made them crawl. The same for all these young wankers who hang around all day and vandalise phone booths at night.

The *Police Secours* phone number is eventually answered by an unenthusiastic police officer who promptly asks him where he is calling from before hanging up on him. He does call back though. This, he explains, is current policy to deal with practical jokers. A practical joker? Aimable, a practical joker? It's them who have to be joking.

Out there, near the body, the ring of gulls is tightening in. In a while, the boldest will rip out a piece of flesh and trigger the squawky scramble for the spoils. If them stupid cops don't get a move on, there will only be bones left to see...

A train crawls slowly across the metal bridge, steel grinding against steel. The lit-up windows neatly outline the cosily seated passengers. Further down, grey warships are barely visible against the equally grey sky and water. Near the Pont Saint Christophe, small boats are lazily riding at anchor in the channel current. The Boulevard Normandie-Niemen running alongside the river Scorff is deserted, the silence only broken by the occasional car swishing by on the wet tarmac.

Suddenly, things get moving. First comes the white police car with its blue emergency rotating light and howling two-tone siren closely followed by the red firemen's van, hurtling down on ill-treated tyres, and then, bringing up the rear, the ambulance.

Aimable chuckles bitterly. An ambulance, the idiots have brought an ambulance! For a stiff that's already half gobbled-up by the winkles. His face takes on an even uglier expression than usual at the thought of such waste. Oh, they're not too concerned about undue expenses… like all those who aren't the payers.

The coppers approach. There are two uniformed men and this woman. What's this bird doing with the cops? She approaches Aimable Maugracieux.

'Detective constable Mary Lester. Is it you who phoned?'

Dumbfounded, Aimable mumbles a *yes*. A female copper! Whatever next?

'Where's the body?'

Aimable nods towards the mud flat.

'Out there.''You haven't touched anything have you?'

'No.'

'Fine, let's go.'

The woman copper turns around to give out her instructions. The firemen get a stretcher out of their van whilst the ambulance men light up a cigarette and lean back against their ambulance. There's no way they're going to plod through the mud in their nice clean uniforms.

Practical-minded, the detective constable (What *do* you call them when they're female? Constableresses?) pulls plastic carrier bags over her shoes. The uniformed men don't take the trouble and are soon up to their ankles in it, swearing under their breath. There's going to be some serious shoe cleaning at the police station that evening.

Aimable ambles along, telling them in a few rough words how he found the body. Mary soon realises that there's no evidence left to find. She signals to the firemen that they can get on with it. The body is hoisted onto the stretcher, its stiffened and therefore unbendable arms splayed out on both sides, and late Maurice Toussaint heads for the morgue.

Aimable is about to go home when the woman cop calls out: 'You're coming with us, sir.'

Aimable jibs.

'But…'

'You've told us everything, I know, but I need to take down your statement.' And, reassuring: 'It won't take long.'

It won't take long. Well that's a good one. Half an hour he's been stuck in the police station waiting room. And for what? To say he went out to check his boat's mooring before the spring tides and that, on his way back, he'd suddenly fancied a few winkles to start his supper with. That was all he had to say… well, not quite. He could've added that he thought it was an absolute shame, yes a shame, that tramps' bodies were to be found right in the city centre.

*

'So, you knew the victim,' asks Mary Lester, playing with her ball pen. *Click, click, click…* goes the pen as she pushes the button in and out. This both irritates and fascinates Aimable. His eyes are riveted to her hands *click, click, click…* He starts, and grumbles: 'I knew him... I knew him... hang on a minute! What did you say his name was?'

'Toussaint. Maurice Toussaint.'

'That's right. And the others called him Winklestar.'

'What others?'

'Well... his pals... You know... I mean the other guys he chatted with on the shore.'

'What guys?'

'I don't know. Guys from the Arsenal, or from the foundry... Quite a few of them own a small boat. Winklestar used to pick winkles, that's where he got his nickname from. Sometimes he gave people a hand to haul in a boat and they brought him a drink. That's all.'

Mary Lester looks at him straight in the eyes.

'Are you sure?'

'Sure of what?' says Maugracieux, exasperated.

'Sure that's all.'

'Well, that's just what I've told you, isn't it!' *Click, click, click*... (Is she *ever* going to stop with that bloody ball pen? She's really getting on my nerves).

'Did he help you?'

Maugracieux flares up.

'Never! I don't need help from people like that.'

'But you did speak with him, didn't you?'

'Never, I tell you. Guys like that, well, I... I...'

Mary Lester waits for him to finish his sentence. *Click, click, click*... As nothing is coming, she asks:

'What do you mean by *guys like that*?'

'Well, you know,' splutters Maugracieux, 'tramps...'

'You don't like them, do you?'

'Can't stand 'em,' spits out Maugracieux. 'Dirty drunken parasites, filth, they ought to be… to be…'

He's stuttering with indignation.

Slyly, Mary helps him on. 'To be what, Monsieur Maugracieux? Shot?'

Suddenly grasping the abysses looming ahead, Maugracieux rapidly shifts into reverse. 'Hang on a minute, don't you go putting words into my mouth.'

Click, click, click…

'I'm not, Monsieur Maugracieux. You said it.'

'I didn't say anything of the sort.' Flustered, Maugracieux adds: 'all I said was that I couldn't stand them and that…'

'And that what?' unrelentlessly probes Mary Lester.

'That it shouldn't be allowed. There!'

'That's not very far from getting rid of them…'

'Wait a minute,' says Maugracieux rising from his chair, 'I haven't killed no one!'

'We'll check, Monsieur Maugracieux.'

'Do you mean you actually suspect me? But the bloke probably just drowned himself. Half the time he was blind drunk anyhow. He could easily have slipped in the mud.'

'We'll check,' repeats Mary Lester.

'If I'd have known groans Maugracieux, would I have turned a blind eye and steered clear of him! At this time, I'd have been nice and cosy at home. These tramps are a bloody nuisance, even dead they're nothing but trouble.'

Mary Lester doesn't react to this last comment of Aimable Maugracieux. She seems to be day-dreaming. Discreetly hiding a yawn behind her right hand, she adds:

'You may go home now, Monsieur Maugracieux. Could you please sign this for me?'

'What's that,' asks Aimable suspiciously.

'It's not your death sentence, just your statement. Do check it out first if you want.'

'You bet I'm going to read it first,' says Maugracieux fishing a ridiculous pair of tiny metal-rimmed glasses out of his pocket and perching them on the end of his strawberry shaped nose.

In fact, he reads the whole thing through twice, just to make sure they haven't put words in his mouth that he might regret later.

'Is this correct?' asks Mary Lester.

The confused rumble that emanates from Maugracieux and resembles a not very complimentary answer could also serve as an agreement. He bends over and, sticking the tip of his tongue out in the effort, painstakingly applies his carefully ornate signature on the form in front of him. Then, head slightly tilted sideways, he contemplates his work with a satisfied grin and, handing the ball pen back to Mary, asks: 'Will that be all?'

'Yes Monsieur Maugracieux. That will be all. Thank you very much for your cooperation.'

'You're welcome,' grumbles Maugracieux, shrugging his shoulders.

He makes for the door sideways, like a crab, and disappears from the scene.

CHAPTER II

'Wow!' says detective constable Mary Lester to the sergeant who's been laboriously typing out Maugracieux' statement with two fingers, 'talk about sweet mouthed! Aimable, on top of that he's called Aimable[Tr. Note], I don't believe it.'

Mary Lester can't know that Désiré Maugracieux, father of the above-mentioned, and his wife Anne, born Dagorn, tried to compensate for their unfortunate patronymic by giving their only child a first name they thought comely. Unfortunately, with his constantly surly air, Maugracieux has been bearing his first name like a cross for the past fifty-nine years.

'Aimable Maugracieux...'

Mary Lester is reading the statement out loud.

'Age fifty-nine, married to Francine Le Gallou. No children (thank God for that, at least the line will soon be extinct), retired 2nd-class master gunner. Indochina, Algeria,... Distinguishing feature: nil... Nil, my eye!' says Mary Lester, 'I would have written: *distinguishing feature: loves no one* or, better still, *hates everybody*! That's it, *hates every-*

Tr. Note : *"In French,* "aimable" *means "pleasant, polite, amiable" whereas* "maugracieux" *is old French for "unpleasant, disagreeable".*

body. That's an eminently distinguishing feature.'

'Not regulatory Miss,' says the sergeant from behind his typewriter.

'You're right Le Moal.' Mary Lester gets up. 'It's not… Pity, though.'

*

Mary Lester is alone in her office, absent-mindedly playing with her ball pen, *clic, click, click*, when the door bursts open on Marc Amedeo. Startled, Mary drops her pen, much to the newcomer's delight.

'Did I scare you then, love?' he asks, grinning insincerely.

Mary Lester doesn't answer. She loathes the man, this detective inspector who is supposed to help her, the rank amateur… She loathes the way he barges into her office without knocking, the way he addresses her as "love" when love has certainly nothing to do with her feelings for this Mediterranean heartbreaker, not to say pimp, who obviously expects all women to swoon at the very sight of his lordship. However, he is her superior and she has to put on a good face. So, she tries…

'Tell me, love, what's this about a stiff turning up last night?' he asks, casually perching himself on the corner of her desk.

Mary Lester pushes her chair back and opens a drawer. She takes out the report Le Moal had typed and starts to read out loud in a monotonous tone: 'The man was called Maurice Toussaint, also known as "Mo" or "Winklestar", take your pick. Age: fifty-five. Profession: tramp.'

'Has he been formally identified?'

'Yes Monsieur. Everybody knew him. He was one of the local characters. He'd set up his quarters in an old blockhouse, under the railway bridge, between rue Camille Pelletan and the Arsenal wall. Apparently a harmless bugger.'

'Good old Winklestar. So, he finally went and got himself drowned.'

'Because you knew him?'

'You'd have trouble finding someone who didn't know him,' says Amedeo. 'In fact, everyone was wondering when he was going to fall in the river. It's a miracle it hasn't happened earlier!'

'He fell in, or was thrown in, or pushed in.'

'Wow there! Hold your horses!' says Amedeo as he stands up. 'We'll just stick with the first option if you don't mind, love. He's been picked up blotto so many times, he most probably shoved himself in the water all on his own like a big boy. He probably tried to use the railway gangplank, despite the warning, and, now the guardrail's gone…'

'Maybe. One thing's sure, he's dead. And another thing that's sure is that he drowned. The autopsy reports there was water in his lungs.'

'You've already got the autopsy report?' says Amedeo, surprised. 'Oh well, things are pretty quiet, I guess our forensic surgeon didn't have much work on his hands. Anyhow… what else?'

'The water in his lungs was brackish…'

'Yes, well, it would, obviously,' says Amedeo impatiently. 'Is that all?'

‘A few none too clean wounds on his wrists and feet and a large bruise on his sternum. The forensic also mentions a 1.20 g blood alcohol level. This, however, doesn't necessarily mean he was drunk. If I believe our records, he's often been picked up with 3 grams so, for him, one gram twenty is practically sober level. On top of that he had a nearly full litre of wine in his bag.’

‘Any money?’

‘Forty-eight francs in his trouser pocket. A fortune for a guy like him. If his death resulted from a quarrel among tramps, his assailant would have rifled his pockets before chucking him in the river.’

‘And would also have taken the bottle of wine.’

‘Probably.’

‘Well then, love?’

‘Well then what, Monsieur?’

‘What do you think of it?’

‘All seems to point towards an accident, however…’

Amedeo frowns.

‘However?’

‘However, I believe it might be wise to wait a few days before closing the case. Just in case something turns up.’

‘Something turns up? Do you really believe that?’

‘Well, Monsieur, you never know. Someone might have seen him fall… another tramp… Who knows? He wasn't alone all the time.’

‘No, he wasn't alone all the time. In fact, I can even tell you he was married.’

‘Married? Well, that's a bit of a surprise Monsieur.’

'Well, when I say married, I mean living in sin... living with a *partner* is probably the politically-correct expression. With *Titine, Titine apple-face*. It's a nickname of course. After her complexion. The red wine... As for her family name, you'll have to ask the hospital.'

'Because she's in hospital?'

'Yes Mademoiselle, has been for the past fortnight. On her last bender, she fell asleep under the van of a fish wholesaler in Keroyan. The man drove off without seeing her and crushed both her legs. Talk about drunkard's luck. Anyone else would have been killed. Not Titine. Two broken legs and she's in clover at the hospital, full board at the taxpayer's expense. Let me tell you, the poor guy who ran her over was hauled over the coals good and proper before the ambulance carried her away. Titine's language is something else!'

'So we can't rely on her testimony'.

'Neither hers nor anyone else's. Believe me, Lester, the world of down-and-outs is as closed as a clam. Particularly where coppers are concerned. If you think they're going to come forward to testify, you've got another think coming, love. We can wait, of course, if you want. Winklestar's in his box at the morgue. He's in no hurry... Neither are we. But the sooner you file the case, the earlier we'll be rid of it.'

Amedeo stretches and yawns.

'Oh well, we'll wait a few days if you want. There's no rush! And, as there's no rush, you can go to the Lanester station. Do you know where it is?'

Mary sighs. Yes, she does know. Rue Marcel Sembat, number 65. She's already been sent there three times and the only crime she's had to fight was severe boredom. This imbecile is probably going to add that she ought to see how a small local station works.

Sure enough, Amedeo adds sententiously: 'You ought to see how a small local station works.'

*

Mary Lester is alone at the reception desk of the Lanester police station. Squatting on the left bank of the Scorff, facing Lorient, Lanester is the working class suburb of the great Western harbour. The current crisis in the shipbuilding and foundry industries, traditional sources of employment in the Lanester area, has sent unemployment rates soaring sky high. The city centre, completely renovated, is rather attractive but the neighbouring streets are full of mean little jerry-built houses, each with its vegetable patch and cement posts strung with wire where laundry is trying to dry.

After dumping her here, detective inspector Marc Amedeo has left just like he had arrived, gustily, leaving her to cope with whatever petty larceny might turn up. Mary's seething. If anything important turns up, it's bound to go to the Lorient central station.

Occupying the ground floor of a modern building, the Lanester police station is stuck between a veterinary practise and a bank. If it weren't for the *Wanted* signs stuck on the wall with their sinister looking mugshots, we could be in any administrative office. Not a uniform in sight. The station is manned by two plain-clothed inspectors who are there to register complaints and transfer them to the Lorient central station.

Mary Lester is sitting at the reception desk. One of the two inspectors has gone out on an investigation requested by the examining magistrate. The other is in his office. He's typing a report. Mary can hear the typewriter 's irregular clicking.

She is definitely bored stiff. She's read the paper through and through. Even the football section, the horse-racing column and the death notices. How desperate can you get!

Maurice Toussaint's death is featured in the miscellaneous section:

MAN FOUND DEAD IN THE SCORFF: the body of a man was found on Thursday at approximately half past four pm, on the Scorff mud flat, at the level of the East India Company's log dock. Maurice Toussaint was fifty-five years old, jobless, originally from Priziac in the Morbihan region. Well known by the police, Maurice Toussaint lived on the fringes of society, in a last world war blockhouse under the Lanester railway bridge. An autopsy has been requested to determine the cause of death.

Mary wearily closes the paper.

The doorbell rings.

'Come in!' shouts Mary.

A young woman enters. She's blond and in obvious distress.

Mary stands up.

'Bonjour Madame.'

'Bonjour,' the young woman answers, vaguely nodding her head in a semi salute.

She looks around her like a hunted animal.

Well, she's not feeling too great, thinks Mary. 'Do sit down,' she says, indicating the chair opposite her, on the other side of the desk.

'Thank you' whispers the woman, perching herself on the very edge of the chair. Then, after a while, in a choked voice: 'I am Madame Sallabert.'

'And what brings you here, Madame Sallabert?'

The woman looks at Mary uneasily.

'You… You are in the police?'

'Yes. Detective constable Mary Lester.'

The woman says: 'Ah!' She seems completely lost.

'You weren't expecting a policewoman?'

'Well… No…'

'As you see,' says Mary cheerily in an attempt to reassure the woman, 'we don't only exist in films.'

The woman lets out a deep sigh.

'In a way, I prefer that. You see, Mademoiselle, my husband has disappeared.'

Mary instantly perks up and asks eagerly: 'Since when, Madame Sallabert?'

'Last Monday, the 16th, that's four days ago.'

'And he didn't say anything when he left?'

'No.'

'He didn't leave a note?'

'No.'

'And when did you see him for the last time?'

'Monday evening. He came home from work a bit earlier than usual, around half past five. He had tea with the kids who had just returned from school and then he left with the shop's van. He had his wellies on and took a chainsaw with him. He said he was going to cut some wood around Kerhervy.'

'Wood?'

'Yes. We have a large fireplace, you see. Since last October's storm, there's firewood laying about all over the place, just waiting to be chopped and taken away. Antoine finds… found…'

She dabs her eyes with her screwed up handkerchief, then, overcoming her emotion: 'He finds it does him good to exercise after work, after all the pressure at the shop.'

'I see,' says Mary politely.

She picks up her ball pen.

'So, his name is Sallabert, Antoine. Age?'

'36.'

'Profession?'

'Sales executive. He's the manager of the CenterMarket.'

Yes. Mary knows the place. It's that huge hypermarket in the middle of Lanester. A bit young, this Antoine Sallabert, to be at the head of such a large store.

'Address?'

'Villa Gwenaël, Toulbahado.'

'Have you been living in Lanester for long?'

'Just over a year. Fourteen months to be precise.'

'Do you have any children?'

This immediately prompts Madame Sallabert to burst into tears. When the bout is finished, she dabs her eyes again and says in a choked voice: 'Sorry. I have two children. A seven-year old boy, Gwenaël, and a girl, Caroline. She's four.'

Mary duly notes all this.

'Are any of his things missing?'

'What do you mean?'

'I mean, has he taken any clothes with him, like if he was going on a journey?'

'No, not at all.'

'Are you sure?'

'Absolutely. When he does go, it's always me who packs his suitcase.'

'Does he go away often?'

'Every month. He has to go up to Paris for his business, the central purchasing agency, meetings... He was there again last week.'

'I see ... Does he have any enemies?'

'Enemies?' she repeats, disconcerted by the question. 'Well ... You know, the arrival of the new hypermarket didn't please everybody... Those who were there before, the small shops... But from there to...'

She doesn't complete her sentence.

It's true, thinks Mary, in this world of cut-throat competition, if people went around shooting all the opposition, there'd be blood all over the place. Anyhow, no hypermarket ever closed just because the manager's gone missing. Managers aren't exactly few and far between.

'Has he been threatened in any way?'

'Not that I know. The front of the store was covered with graffiti two or three times, but that happens everywhere...'

'Yes, that's true,' says Mary, still writing. 'Err... does he have a mistress?'

The word mistress triggers another bout of tears that Madame Sallabert tries to stifle in her handkerchief. Embarrassed, Mary Lester tries to mitigate the brutality of her question.

'I'm sorry Madame Sallabert, but I *do* have to explore all possibilities.'

'Of course,' she says screwing up her hankie into a tight ball. I don't know... He has been coming home rather late these days... And he has been a bit strange... But, quite frankly, I don't know!'

Yes, wives are usually the last to know about their husband's escapades thinks Mary.

'Does he have life-insurance?'

'I think he does. He has talked to me about one, but I'll have to look at his papers. He takes care of all those things...'

Tears are welling up again, maybe at the thought of having to cope with all that alone if hubby doesn't come back.

'Does your husband have any friends outside from work?'

'Not really. You see, we've only been here a year so we haven't made any friends yet but Antoine does play with the Lanester football club. I suppose he's made a few acquaintances there but he never says much about them. What he does talk about is the judo club he wants to start here, in Lanester.'

'Ah, he does judo?'

'Oh yes, judo is his passion. He's a third Dan black belt. He even belonged to the French army team during his military service.'

'He did?... Now, why didn't you tell us earlier that's he'd disappeared?'

'I don't know... I guess I didn't want to make a fuss... And then, if he comes back with a plausible explanation, I'm going to look a right fool.'

Mary Lester nods encouragingly.

'You know,' continues Madame Sallabert, 'when someone disappears... Tell me, you must know about these things, is there a normal time span before one should report a missing person?'

'Ah! well, that's a poser. I suppose everyone reacts differently. I don't think there's any set rule. I suppose people tend to react faster when it's a child...'

She stands up, smiles, and tries to look reassuring.

'Anyhow I shouldn't worry too much if I were you. As you say, your husband is probably going to turn up today or tomorrow with a good reason for his absence. In the meantime, given what you've just told me, I'll begin a discreet investigation. Oh, by the way, can you give me a photo of your husband?'

Madame Sallabert opens her handbag.

'Here, I brought three...'

Mary Lester looks at the photos handed to her. She sees a proud father holding the hand of a little boy gazing up at him, eyes lost in admiration. On the second photo, the entire Sallabert family stares at her and Mary notes that, although of average height, Madame Sallabert outweighs her husband in size by half a head. He isn't tall, Antoine Sallabert, neither tall nor fat. A pocket-sized man!

'Try not to worry too much,' says Mary Lester walking Madame Sallabert to the door, 'I'll keep you informed.'

CHAPTER III

'My, my, you are a busy little bee!'

The tone is ironic. Hands stuck in his trouser pockets, mackintosh flapping, his felt hat shadowing his eyes, cigarette stuck to his upper lip, Marc Amedeo fancies himself as Bogart revisited. With a superior air, he squats squarely in front of Mary Lester's metal desk.

Mary tries to look composed but she's sure her eyes will betray her. She is really fed up with this arrogant self-opinionated macho and his condescending airs...

'That was Madame Sallabert,' she answers in what she hopes is a neutral tone. 'You know her, of course'.

Amedeo whirls round, mack tails flying.

'Of course I know her. In fact, I know all the pretty ladies' he says ingratiatingly as he stretches a nicotine fingered hand towards her cheek, as if to stroke her. Mary starts back as if approached by a snake. Surprised, Amedeo freezes, looking rather silly with his hand stuck in mid-air. He lets out an asinine laugh.

'Now, now, young lady, don't be scared, I'm not going to eat you up.'

'I'm not scared,' says Mary icily, eyes still riveted on the hand stretched out towards her.

Marc Amedeo lets his arm drop and sits down on the chair just vacated by Madame Sallabert. Leaning backwards and taking on what he believes is an inspired expression, he tries to blow smoke rings.

If he could see the idiotic picture he's making with his small pursed mouth, thinks Mary, *he'd quit smoking. Honestly, what a nerd! I suppose he fancies he's got a chance with me?*

Marc Amedeo gives up on the smoke-ring display.

'And what did dear Madame Sallabert want?'

'Not a lot. She just wanted to report that her husband has disappeared.'

Marc Amedeo sits up suddenly.

'Well, well! Come on love, tell us all.'

Love! Why not darling while he's at it! Mary breathes in deeply and tries to keep calm.

'Monday evening,' she reads out from her notebook, 'Antoine Sallabert left in one of his shop's vans. He told his wife he was going to cut some wood around Kerhervy. Since then, he hasn't reappeared.'

'Is that so,' says Amedeo in a playful tone, 'he's gone walkies… Interesting. Tell me Lester, this Sallabert is the manager of the CenterMarket, isn't he?'

'Yes Monsieur. But why do you say he's gone walkies?'

Amedeo raises his arms to heaven to demonstrate how stupid he finds the question.

'What else do you want it to be, love? A guy leaves home and doesn't come back, not exactly something to write home about! How else would you call it?'

'I don't know Monsieur, but maybe we could consider other hypotheses.'

'Of course we could, Lester, one always can. We could, for instance, consider kidnapping, couldn't we?'

'It does happen,' says Mary defensively.

'Oh yeees!' says Amedeo now frankly ironic. 'It's been known to happen and still will if you want my opinion. Only…' he looks slyly at Mary, 'only, never in Lanester.'

'There's a beginning to everything.'

Amedeo comes back and perches himself on the corner of the desk.

'Tell me Lester, why are people usually kidnapped?'

'For the ransom.'

'Right. For money. For a lot of money in fact. Kidnapping someone and holding his family to ransom is a hazardous enterprise. It can pay a lot, but it can also cost a lot. In court, the jury don't mess around with that sort of offence. The guys who attempt this sort of thing usually belong to organised crime… or to terrorist groups. You name me one person in Lanester rich enough to be worth kidnapping. You name me one gang of criminals sufficiently organised to set up this sort of thing, or one terrorist organisation…'

Mary timidly proffers: 'The *FLB*'.[Tr. Note]

Amedeo shrugs his shoulders.

'Don't make me laugh. That bunch of amateurs are just good enough to paint over road signs

Tr. Note : *The* FLB *(*Front de Libération de la Bretagne*)* *is the "Brittany Liberation Front"* at night-time. And, anyhow, has the family received any request for ransom money?'

'Madame Sallabert didn't mention it,' admits Mary.

'So, that's one line of enquiry we can strike off the menu,' says Amedeo. 'Not that I ever considered it an option mind you. And then, what else?'

'He might have been killed,' ventures Mary.

'Where's the body?' And, Mary remaining silent, 'Show me the body, love. Show me the body and we'll immediately open up an inquiry. In the meantime, we've got quite enough work as it is without inventing extras. We'll cross that bridge if and when we get to it.'

He holds his hand out.

'Give me the file!'

'But...' Mary tries to object.

Amedeo insists.

'I want to look after this personally. I feel you're going to get into trouble. Believe my experience, in cases like this, you want to walk on egg shells. This requires tact!'

'That's just it'

'Just it what? Love'.

'I promised the woman a discreet inquiry.'

'And you did well. Hey, Lester, why are you looking at me like that? Do you think me incapable of discretion?'

Mary imperceptibly shrugs her shoulders and mutters: 'No Monsieur.'

'There's a good girl!'

He stands up, noisily pushing back his chair.

'Follow me young lady. We're going back to Lorient. I've got something for you: three or four delinquents breaking and entering a country house. The ones who were in the house managed to run away across the neighbouring fields but we caught the car driver. After a hairy chase, mind you! Just like in those American films. Luckily, the idiot ended up in a wall. Have you ever interrogated delinquent youths?'

'No Monsieur.'

'Well, this is a good opportunity to start, your maiden flight if I may say!'

*

Mary Lester returns to Lorient, Amedeo hard on her heels. She's been working in Brittany for a year now, and what has she done in a year? Registered complaints for shoplifting, overnight damage, the main victims being overturned dustbins, telephone booths looted for their few francs, vandalized flowerbeds and overclean walls spattered with graffiti, some obscene, some provoking, always vulgar, in which some perverted minds proclaim to see the spontaneous expression of contemporary art.

Ah, yes, there are also the cars or mopeds "borrowed" for one night binges. Fights in cafes or in front of nightclubs, mainly teenage gangs releasing their pent-up energy in brawls instead of using it to find a job.

Once a country village, now the dormitory suburb of its grand neighbour, Lorient, Lanester is a quiet place. There are few high-rise buildings. People here usually come from the farming world and have remained faithful to their detached houses and little gardens where the family veg are grown, alongside a few chickens or rabbits, like in the old days at the ancestral farm, out there, someplace near Pont-Scorff. Carefully cemented pathways are lined with metal washing lines where laundry is drying out in the wind. These are modest folks, who, save a few lucky ones, have never known winter sports or exotic sunny holidays in faraway countries.

Lanester, a small town in France like a thousand others, with the same problems as a thousand others. Town planners have designed a heart for this town, with small neat modern buildings that are probably quite cosy... Large open spaces, a fair-sized lake, a few shops, some hypermarkets, an industrial area like everywhere else and two large companies: the Arsenal, that works for the French Marine, and the SBFM, the "foundry" as it's called here, a subsidiary Renault plant.

A town where nothing happens for months on end and now, in two days, two events: the death by drowning of the tramp Maurice Toussaint and the disappearance of the hypermarket manager, Antoine Sallabert. As far as detective inspector Marcel Amedeo is concerned, these are "non events". The drunken tramp fell in the water (accident - case closed) and the hypermarket manager has just gone walkies. Happens every day.

Mary finds this strange but, after all, it's true, winos drown in France every day and hundreds of people with apparently no more reasons than Antoine Sallabert do vanish into thin air every year. So... Maybe she's getting carried-away, little

Mary Lester. Maybe she's just imagining things through sheer disenchantment? Who knows?

Well, anyhow, detective inspector Marc Amedeo is taking care of it. All Mary Lester has to do is investigate the country house burglary.

*

The youth is sitting in front of Mary Lester, arms resting on his knees, head hanging low. Mary looks at him with a mixture of pity and bitterness. A youth in a police station, what at waste!

He's watching Mary... He'd like to look fierce but only manages to betray his anxiety.

He's wearing the customary black leather jacket, stonewashed jeans and trainers. Is he twenty? Not sure. Mary glances at the report of the police officers who arrested him after the car chase, and its unfortunate end in a wall.

She reads: *Francis Le Gwen, age nineteen, lives in Penher. Appalling school reports. Left school without qualifications, is entering adulthood unemployed.* Yes, that would follow, she thinks.

Mary looks at him again. He looks like a nice enough lad despite his stubborn brow, shifty eyes and clenched fists. In good hands, he could have become a good workman. She spots a few greasy streaks on his hands. Maybe a mechanic...

'Tell me Francis, do you like mechanics?'

The boy's dark stare lights up, surprised by the question. He didn't expect that. First of all, being interrogated by a babe, that's not frequent. She's not bad, that girl. A bit old of course, at least twenty-five, give or take a few years, but still, she's not bad looking. Now that she's taken off her navy-blue duffle coat with its big wooden buttons, you can guess some perfectly feminine shapes under her Aran style jumper. Like him, she's wearing jeans, washed out but clean, with black boots, well polished.

'Why?' he asks.

Mary smiles. Since his arrest, Monsieur Le Gwen hasn't uttered a sound. Apparently, the policemen had a hard time trying to get his identity out of him. Wouldn't say a word, Francis Le Gwen. Not even his name to these fucking coppers. Hard luck! A policeman living in the same neighbourhood had recognised him.

There's no way he's going to squeal and give them his pals' names! But mechanics, well, yes, he is rather keen on mechanics. In fact he knows a lot about mechanics, without having ever learnt. He casts a sidelong glance at Mary Lester. This woman copper is definitely weird.

'You're wondering what mechanics have to do with it, aren't you?' continues Mary.

The boy nods, bemused.

'Well, usually, in a gang, it's the best driver who gets the wheel. And, usually, the best driver is also the best mechanic.'

Francis Le Gwen is now looking straight up at Mary Lester, nearly all trace of hostility has vanished from his face. It's true that, as far as driving is concerned, he's definitely the best in the gang... But, he failed, well and truly. It wasn't his fault if the right rear wheel of this fucking van jammed when you braked!

'And so you had no problem to start it…'
'Why would I?'
The question fuses spontaneously, with a touch of sarcasm.
'Well,' says Mary, 'without the keys… When I forget my car keys, mate, I'm stuck! But of course, for a specialist like you, that's no problem.'
The bitch! So that's what she's leading on to. She's trying to nail him with car theft. That's why she's been beating around the bush. Those bastards are all the same, male or female.
'Hey, hang on there!' he shouts out, 'I didn't pick no lock. That car, we found it near the Pont du Bonhomme, in a restaurant car park. It was open, with the keys dangling from the dashboard.'
As Mary Lester is eying him dubiously, he cries out, raising his right hand: 'Honest, all we wanted was to have a drink but they chucked us out. There was a posh wedding going on inside, or so they said. So we wanted to go back to Lanester. It was pissin' down and we didn't want to walk so we borrowed the van. Only Petit…'
Shit! Francis Le Gwen nearly mentioned a name. Once you start yapping… His older pals have warned him, the ones who've already been in the nick: with coppers, you just shut your big mouth. Otherwise, they always find some way of screwing you.
So he clams up like an oyster.
Marc Amedeo walks in behind him. Le Gwen doesn't hear him enter. He grabs the youth by the collar and spins him round. 'Carry on Francis. Petit what? I didn't hear the full name properly so, come on, let's have it!' He shakes the boy until his

teeth rattle and, irked by the boy's silence, goes wild: 'You little bastard! So, you won't say anything! Well we'll soon see about that.'

Shocked by this brutal intervention, Mary Lester comes forward: 'But Monsieur…'

Enraged, Marc Amadeo turns around towards her without letting go of Francis Le Gwen.

'But what, detective constable Mary Lester, just out of training six months ago. Are you going to teach me my job? Are you going to tell me how to handle these little bastards? Hey? I suppose you're going to start blabbing about psychology or some other bullshit? I'll tell you the only language they understand: a good old wallop and a kick up the arse. That's how you talk to scum like this.'

Mary tries to resist with dignity: 'I thought you said I was in charge of this cross-examination.'

'Yeah, well,' growls Amedeo, his mouth distorted with anger, 'I said. So what? We all make mistakes, don't we? Well, you're not in charge any more. Happy? No? I don't give a fuck. I'm the boss here. The way you're going about it, we'll still be here tomorrow. Get out! *Monsieur* and I have things to talk about, from man to man.'

Honestly, what an arsehole! Disgusted, Mary gathers her things and leaves, not without a friendly wink to Le Gwen who looks worried stiff.

*

Mary slams the door violently; it's the only way she can vent her feelings and she's jolly well going to use it.

Sergeant Le Moal, a rather sweet pot-bellied old man, red-faced with grey hair, is tending reception and has heard everything. He's the oldest cop of the station and is due for retirement at the end of the year. He'll at last be able to devote himself fully to his garden and the games of *boules* with his pals.

He rather likes the Lester kid and he's sad to see her upset.

'Come on, Mademoiselle,' he says paternally (he never could call this kid, younger than his eldest daughter, "detective constable"), 'not to worry. He's not completely wrong, Amadeo, these young delinquents aren't easy to handle.'

He squirms a bit in his chair, embarrassed. Dare he say it? He dares: 'It's not a job for a woman.'

'And what *is* a woman's job then?' asks Mary aggressively.

'Well, I don't know…' says Le Moal, 'my daughter for instance, she teaches French…'

And is Le Moal proud of his daughter! Mary softens up. She approaches the desk behind which the sergeant looks caged in.

'In the police, Le Moal, what is a woman's job in the police?'

'Well…' says Le Moal uneasy.

Mary flares up again.

'You don't know, do you? Well I don't either. After all, maybe there isn't any job for women in the police force.'

'I didn't say that, Mademoiselle,' protests Le Moal weakly.

‘That's true, you didn't say it, but I'm discovering it. It's become a daily issue. A tramp drowned? Just a silly accident, a sort of natural death. Just drop it, Lester. Monsieur Sallabert has disappeared? He's just gone walkies, love. Marc Amadeo, the Great Marc Amadeo will personally take care of the investigation. Cars stolen by delinquent youths, attempted burglaries, that's not for trainee detective constable Lester either.’ She glares at the sergeant through the perplex screen. ‘So tell me, Le Moal, what's left for trainee detective constable Lester?’

As the unfortunate sergeant remains silent, eyes cast down, she carries on: ‘I know, I'm going to investigate the blisters on detective inspector Amedeo's hands!’

Not missing this opportunity of changing subjects, Le Moal laughs. ‘Blisters? On Amedeo's hands? Are you sure you took a good look at them, Mademoiselle?’

‘You bet I did,’ says Mary. ‘I had his hand waved under my nose long enough to memorise every inch of its skin.’

‘Maybe he's taken up DIY after all,’ comments Le Moal, sceptical. ‘That might be why he's in such a bad mood.’

‘Who knows?’ says Mary. And, on a more professional tone: ‘Do you know where the wrecked car is?’

‘Which one? The delinquents'?’

‘Yep.’

Le Moal studies his register.

‘We had it towed to the Renault garage.’

‘Fine. Thank you Le Moal.’

She makes for the door, Le Moal's eyes following her. He seems puzzled, obviously thinking *Now what's she up to?* Mary pushes the heavy metal door with it's armoured glass pane and leaves.

The fog is spreading, gradually erasing the grey houses. Mary Lester breathes in a deep gush of water-saturated air. As she's been kicked out of her office, she's going for a walk. Not just any walk, mind you, a stroll over to the Renault garage, for instance.

CHAPTER IV

The van has been dumped in a corner of the yard, already cluttered by a variety of other wrecks. It's a beige Renault Traffic high-top with the company name in bold blue letters on both sides: *Lanester CenterMarket.*

The right wing is completely bashed in and the force of the impact has ejected the passenger seat. Francis Le Gwen can thank his lucky star he came out of it without a scratch. He must have been stunned though. He was still slumped over the steering wheel when the cops nabbed him.

A workman creeps in behind Mary Lester and says, joking:

'You want to buy it?'

He's unlucky. Mary is definitely not in a joking mood. She's fed up to the teeth with these blokes who think that, just because she's a woman, they're entitled to tease her. She draws her card out like a gun.

'Police!'

The word always makes an impression. The mechanic stops, dumbfounded.

'Oh, sorry.'

'Did you examine this vehicle?'

'No. I'm not in charge of that sort of thing, its...'
Mary interrupts.
'It doesn't matter. Can you tell me if it's been jumpstarted?'
'I can always have a look.'
He opens the driver's door and dives under the wheel. 'Nope, hasn't been touched,' he says straighttening himself up again. 'The wiring's clean.'
'Are you sure?'
'Well yes. See for yourself. Anyhow, why should anyone jumpstart it? The keys are in it.'
So, on this point at least, Le Gwen didn't lie.
The mechanic looks at her, puzzled. 'Is that all I can do for you?'
'That's all, thank you.'
He walks away, slowly, looking back at her twice. He still doesn't understand. Mary gets in the van and goes in the back. The high-top allows her to stand up. The metal-sheet floor is covered with a sheet of plywood. Not an ounce of sawdust or bark. Antoine Sallabert never carted any wood in here, not recently at least. On the other hand... Mary bends down. This grey dust... it looks like cement. Freshly made cement which has overflowed and, here, these scratches on the plywood... a rusty circle, as if a heavy round-shaped object had stood there. That's all. Otherwise, the van is absolutely empty.
'So, detective constable Lester, where's all this leading you?'
Startled, Mary jumps, inspector Amedeo's disagreeable voice pulling her from her thoughts. She hasn't heard him creeping up behind her. Oh, how she hates this obnoxious git!

Inspector Amadeo is not pleased. Not pleased at all. Who had the brainy idea of shoving this little smartarse on him? A little smartarse who is poking her nose all over the place. Of course, he doesn't say this out loud, as crudely, but that's what he's thinking. He's thinking it so hard, it shows, it's written all over his sullen face.

He's fiddling with a ruler between his nicotine stained fingers and the ruler is about to break. Mary Lester is standing to attention in front of the desk which he is battering with his other fist. She looks at him straight in the eye, unblinkingly, sure she's within her rights. Because, come on, what harm was she doing examining the stolen van? It might be pointless, OK, maybe... But from there to getting this mad, it's ridiculous.

Later on, when she has left, Marc Amedeo will really fly off the handle, damning the entire female population, particularly the nosey bitches who meddle with police affairs. And also, for good measure, the eejits who had the bloody stupid idea of opening the profession to the weaker sex. He will even call the sentry to witness and the latter will laugh obsequiously.

'You don't really believe,' says Mary icily, 'that I worked three years to get my masters degree in law, plus the police training, just to type reports in some remote police station?'

Amadeo wearingly puts the ruler back on his desk. Now that he's let his anger fly, he's nearly able to speak calmly. Or at least, he tries. Spreading both hands, palm down on the desk blotter, looking straight into Mary eyes, he says:

'Listen love, what the hell do you care whether this bloody van has transported a sack of cement, a metal drum, carrots, turnips or whatever? Just tell me. What the hell do you care? This van is a commercial vehicle which has probably carted around just about all the items for sale in the supermarket. If you want a full inventory, you haven't finished. And, to come back to my initial question, where does it lead us?'

'It might lead us nowhere,' persists Mary, 'but I really don't see why you blow your top just because I went to the Renault garage to look up the van.'

'Waste of time,' growls Amadeo. 'We've got better things to do.'

'Speak for yourself. You're taking care of the tramp, you're taking care of the delinquent youths, you're taking care of Sallabert's disappearance...' And she nearly adds: *and you probably wouldn't mind taking care of little Madame Sallabert herself. But you're too old, too ugly and too bloody hopeless. You wouldn't stand a chance.*

But that would be pushing things too far. It's probably true, but some things are better left unsaid. So, she continues, out loud:

'All the same, we should have found that chainsaw in Antoine Sallabert's van.'

'Oh! that's what you were looking for?' Marc Amadeo suddenly seems relieved. 'Well then, be happy young lady, we've found that chainsaw.'

Mary asks, eagerly: 'Ah! Where?'

'In a door, strangely enough.'

She stares at Amedeo. Is he taking the mickey

again? But no. Amadeo is much more relaxed now. He even seems to be enjoying himself.

'Yes, Mademoiselle Lester. In the door of the house your little friend and his bunch of angels were trying to break into. You see, they didn't have the keys and the oak door was eight centimetres thick. Never mind. These tough guys weren't impressed. Four slashes with the chainsaw and, wham bam, no more obstacle. Only, a chainsaw tends to be rather noisy. Even more so in the middle of the night. The neighbours woke up, phoned us, and you know the rest. Are you satisfied?'

Mary shrugs her shoulders and says:

'For all that, we still don't know what happened to Antoine Sallabert.'

Amedeo raises his arms in despair.

'Ah! There we are, Antoine Sallabert has disappeared. He hasn't disappeared for everybody, believe you me.'

'You have news!' cries out Mary.

'No, no, love,' says Amadeo tapping the side of his nose with his finger, I just have a good nose, a copper's nose. Plus twenty years of experience. If Francis Le Gwen was telling the truth, he'd admit, I'd put my head on the block, that they found the van at the train station or at the airport… '

'But,' objects Mary, 'he said…'

'I know,' interrupts Amedeo, 'he says he found the van in the restaurant car park, near the Pont du Bonhomme[Tr. Note]… But I don't believe him. You can reassure little Madame Sallabert as much as you want with your tales but, as far as I'm

Tr. Note : *Literally, old man's bridge.*

concerned, her guy's scarpered. And don't pull such a face love, he's just scarpered with another woman, that's all. It happens every day.'

'But he didn't take any clothes.'

'So what. That doesn't prove anything. He probably had a packed suitcase ready at his office, or elsewhere. He tells the wife he's going to chop some wood but, in fact, he nips round to the office and collects his suitcase. He gets changed in the van, catches a plane, or the train —even more anonymous— to Paris and, once there, well, the world is his. Quite a common tale. He probably took a life insurance policy to his wife's benefit and in six months, or a year, or three, he'll turn up in the Galapagos or Tuamotu islands living it up on a sunny sand beach. Or he won't turn up at all because he'll have been just that little bit cleverer than most. It's happened before and it'll happen again.'

'That's rotten,' says Mary Lester.

'No it isn't,' says Amedeo, now perfectly calm, 'It's life, that's all. Do you know how many people disappear in France each year, people with no more reason than Sallabert to vanish into thin air? No? Twenty-five thousand! Twenty-five thousand individuals, male and female, who just disappear like that, pfuitt, and who are never heard of again. So, you see, your Sallabert just makes one more.'

'But,' protests Mary, 'his wife is charming.'

'Of course she's charming. For outsiders, she's even very charming. But who tells you she isn't an absolute pain at home? Hey? We don't know. You are single aren't you? Ah! You don't realise how lucky you are. I too have a charming wife but sometimes… sometimes… don't I wish…'

He drifts off dreamingly, then wipes his brow and sighs wearily.

'Leave me now, love, I've got things to do.'

*

Mary finds herself standing in the police station hallway. Sergeant Le Moal is sitting at the reception; on the tip of his large red nose a tiny pair of half-moon spectacles is perched, *his reading glasses* as he calls them. For the time being, he's working hard on the crosswords that seem to be particularly challenging today. Looking up over his glasses, he gently asks Mary:

'Are you all right, Mademoiselle?'

'This just isn't my day Le Moal,' says Mary, 'I don't know what I've done to Amedeo, honestly, that guy's a real misogynist!'

'Probably unhappy at home,' says Le Moal in a confidential tone, an expert's tone. He bends over the counter, looks right and left to check that the corridors are empty, and whispers: 'You don't know his wife?'

'No, nobody ever sees her.'

'A very pretty lady,' says Le Moal, drawing out generous forms in the air with both hands. 'They say she's twenty years younger than him. They also say… he places two fingers on each side of his head, like horns, and takes on a leery look.'

Mary chuckles.

'Amedeo, that macho, is a cuckold?'

Le Moal nods.

'And he knows it too. If you ask me, for him to be in such a rotten mood, he probably caught her in the act. That's probably why he's such a pain today.' And, strangely, as if to excuse his superior's behaviour, he adds: 'Well, put yourself in his shoes.'

Mary giggles again.

'No thank you, I'd rather not if you don't mind.'

'Apart from that,' concludes Le Moal without catching onto the irony of Mary's answer, 'apart from that, he's not a bad sort really.'

*

Mary leaves the police station and gets into her car. So, Amedeo's a cuckold… Strangely enough, the news rather pleases her. She feels revenged… Revenged by another woman, a woman she doesn't even know. Marc Amedeo has just been so loathsome today that she really would have liked to smash his face up. For instance, she could have tried out a few of the close combat moves she was taught in her training. Unfortunately, there are things that are just not done.

She drives along the empty streets of Lanester in the Mini she brought with her first wages, when she worked for a lawyer, before joining the police. Maybe she should have continued and taken the bar, or else become a magistrate; in juvenile courts for instance, she would have liked that.

Lawyer, judge, those are respectable professions. Who hasn't heard, on the radio or the tele, people taken to court proclaiming, hand to their heart and chin proudly jutting out: *I have faith in the justice of my country!* Have you ever heard anyone say: *I have faith in the police of my country!* No, you haven't. But can you have faith in the police of your country? Are the likes of Marcel Amadeo and his angry outbursts the sort of people you would want to trust?

She slows down. Without realising it, she's arrived at Kerhervy, a place she rather likes, right up the river Blavet. In Summer, there's often quite a crowd here. Behind a wooden stake fence, a strange open air theatre spreads its grassy terraces right down to the water's edge where the stage is set. Great trees are laying there, victim to the terrible October storm. That would probably be where Antoine Sallabert had planned to come and cut some wood. Emerging out of the water, the carcasses of old wooden trawlers are rotting in the mud flat, what's left of their hull reaching for the sky like rows of arms in despair.

In season, the spot is an old favourite for the locals with folk swimming, having a friendly picnic or messing around in canoes. The air is filled with bird song, rustling leaves and the children's squeals of delight.

In winter, it's deserted. But Mary still likes to come here. Some might find the place gloomy but Mary finds it romantic. She likes to watch the black cormorants perched on the remains of the boats, drying their feathers. They stand there, motionless, wings outspread as if crucified. In the twilight, the huts where the spotlights and loudspeakers are hung for shows look like watchtowers and give the outdoor theatre a sinister death camp air.

Mary takes a few steps along the shore. It smells good, real... the sea, the kelp, the forest... She walks back to the stage, long deserted. Works seem to have been started but the site is obviously abandoned. They'll probably resume the job in the spring. On the ground, a light patch. Night is falling. Mary bends down to the grey patch, touches it. It's still fresh and it's... cement!

Mary suddenly shivers and straightens up, anxiety floods her. Nothing romantic about the scenery now. Under the sinister watchtowers, the trawler carcasses look like castles of misery, haunted by maleficent gnomes.

She runs to the Mini, jumps in and slams the door shut. Quick, the key... she fumbles with the sodding key that won't fit in the ignition... Ah, at last, the engine roars, the headlights flood the road, the gearbox moans as she reverses brutally. In her familiar universe, with the smell of the leather seat and her favourite Mozart tape running, Mary calms down.

Nothing has moved, there still isn't anyone in sight. Mary drives towards the city lights and laughs back at her panic.

*

Mary is driving aimlessly through Lanester. The window is rolled down and the damp gentle air is soothing. Why did the dried cement patch trigger such a reaction? Why did all her childhood terrors suddenly flood back, so brutally? At night, when the lights were out in her bedroom, she had been so petrified she dared barely breathe when the garden's big plum tree was metamorphosed into a fantastic monster by the moonlight, when the wind made ghosts out of the curtains.

She passes the Arsenal, following the long grey wall with its barbed wire crown, realising only too late that the road is a dead end, that it leads to the worksite entrance where a gendarme is standing guard in front of the *Military zone, keep out!* board.

The workshops are empty. There is still life at the cafe *Chez Marie-Thé* where workmates are having one for the road before going home.

Turning the car around in the narrow lane is not easy and hearing the quietly ironic gendarme commenting on Mary's efforts to his colleague in the guardhouse doesn't exactly help but she concentrates on finishing her U turn and drives on. She's in no hurry and just turns into whatever street takes her fancy.

Here is the Scorff now, with the wooden stakes sticking out of the mud, the place where Aimable Maugracieux found the unfortunate Winklestar.

Since when have these stakes been there? Some must be over a hundred years old. People say they've been listed as ancient monuments. Why not? Men can always list them, that won't stop the sea from reducing them to nothing. The sea's only limit is called Eternity. Ebb and flow will succeed, again and again, and these remnants of the old navy will gradually disintegrate with the tides, last souvenirs of days when boats were made of wood and wind-powered.

Only a few scholars will remember that this was the place where the East India Company, then surrounded only by moors and mud, had built a formidable two hundred feet long vessel to do business with India and that that was the reason why the city that grew out of this moor was baptised Lorient, the Orient.

On the other side of the estuary, the great city is lighting up. With its strangely regular metal structure and massive stone pillars, the bridge overhangs the estuary. In the distance, a few warships are anchored in the channel, their regulatory grey barely visible against the surrounding greyness.

The little car reaches the bridge. A Paris-bound train rattles by. Through the lit-up windows, the silhouettes of the passengers look like shadow puppets. The red tail lights run off in the dusk and silence falls.

It's been two weeks now that the metal gangway along the railway line has been barred off. The parapet is under repair. Barriers lit up by little lanterns block the way.

Is there a link between these works and the tramp's death? He used to live here, near the bridge, in the old world-war II blockhouse, between rue Camille Pelletan and the Arsenal wall. Maurice Toussaint had a "villa" with a seaview, or should we say a mudview, on the mudflat where a sewer pipe vomited streams of soapy water, with a sordid little garden decorated by wind-blown discarded plastic bags gracing the bare trees with a strange multicoloured foliage, a few rats...

Amedeo's probably right. The tramp's death was an accident. Mary Lester can visualise the scene: Maurice Toussaint picks his winkles and starts for Lorient to sell them. Like every other day, he takes the railway bridge without, of course, taking the slightest notice of the *Danger, work in progress, no entry* sign. Late at night, he comes home the same way, slips and falls in the water...

It's the most plausible hypothesis, the most rational. However, Mary isn't happy with it. Same as she's not happy with Amedeo's theory as to what happened to Antoine Sallabert. She tries to think rationally: would she have the same doubts if these theories were put forward by a friendly colleague. No. To be honest, she has to admit that her violent dislike for Marc Amedeo is not completely foreign to her scepticism.

She would really like to prove this self opinionated ass wrong. Prove that Antoine Sallabert isn't necessarily a bastard who abandoned his wife and kids to go gallivanting.

And, by the way, could he afford it? The hypermarket didn't belong to him; he may be the manager, OK, but he's still only an employee. In these days of massive unemployment, does one drop such a job in a hurry? No, it doesn't make sense.

Mary Lester's ears are still ringing with the words of Marc Amadeo, the cuckolded macho (serve him right): '*He gets changed in the van, catches a plane, or the train...*' And she fantasizes the rest of the dialogue, the final replies she slams at Amadeo:

'*But then, chief, if he got changed in the van, we should have found his worksuit, his wellies... And please Monsieur, don't tell me he took them with him to Tahiti to fish in the lagoon.'*

She sees him getting annoyed. He doesn't like people resisting him. In his obtuse little macho copper's brain, a subordinate who objects just about amounts to rebellion. On top of that, if the trainee is wearing a skirt... She can just imagine his peremptory answer:

'*Someone stole them! The van wasn't locked and anybody could have got in it. Gumboots, a worksuit, nowadays everything's worth nicking.*'

Carried away by her fantasy, Mary Lester answers in a suave tone:

'*And they leave the chainsaw?*'

She can just see Amedeo frowning with his thick bushy eyebrows.

'*What?*'

Mary continues, slowly, as if speaking to a mentally retarded child: '*The potential thief steals the boots, the worksuit, which are not necessarily his size, and leaves the chainsaw which is worth ten times more? That's not rational, boss.*'

She can feel that Amedeo is going to become vulgar. He's running short of arguments and he doesn't like it.

'*Oh Lester, give me a break. You're a pain in the neck. There you are splitting hairs in three. The worksuit, the boots, the thief could have thrown them out of the window couldn't he?*'

And Mary Lester would docilely agree:

'*Yes boss, the thief could have thrown them out of the window. In fact, that's probably what he did.*'
Why didn't she think of that earlier?

And Marc Amadeo would look at her nastily, wondering if by any chance this bloody woman wasn't being sarcastic.

*

Mary climbs up the bridge embankment and walks on the metal gangway that vibrates under her feet. She tries not to look down as, without the parapet, one could easily feel giddy. At last, she reaches a girder, firmly grasps it and bends over. The tide is creeping in on the mudflat, licking the sides of a few small boats. An empty plastic bottle is sailing away in a gust of wind, like a miniature yacht. Pollution is rife. People are lazy and just dump their rubbish any old place without caring. The public rubbish dump is too far and, here, the place is deserted. So they quickly back in their car, open the boot and, Bob's your uncle, no one will know, dump their refuse into the water. That's consumer society for you!

An old bed base is rotting away, its springs sprouting out like intestines, a cooker with its white enamel flanks, a large metal drum, some old car tyres. And good old mother nature is going to gulp all this up, here, in the black mud, and degrade it slowly. Nature is in no hurry, she's got eternity ahead of her.

In a way, Winklestar had also been chucked out by society like a piece of refuse. He falls in the water and dies of shock, or drowning, pick your choice. The ebbing tide slowly pushes his body towards the Pont Saint-Christophe. Then draws it back with its immutable rhythm: six hours in, six hours out. It's been like that since the first day, and there's no reason for it to change.

A one way ticket was enough for Winklestar though. With the strap of his carpet-bag, he moored himself to an ancient stake where Aimable (the ill-named) Maugracieux (the well-named) was to discover him, much to his displeasure.

*

Mary Lester's night is rough. Her dreams are haunted by cement. Gigantic cormorants, with pterodactyl jaws and great staring eyes gawk at her longingly, like the vultures perched on Mexican cactuses eying hanging bodies in cowboy films.

Then the watchtowers move across her room, the black wooden stakes reminding her of crucifixion, high voltage barbed wires... And drowned bodies, lots of laughing drowned bodies with their hollow orbits a mass of winkles.

And that arsehole who shouts at her: '*So, inspector Lester, where's all this leading you?*'

She wakes up panting, soaked in sweat, still mumbling in her nightmare: '*Nowhere, boss, nowhere.*'

The pink glow of her bedside lamp soothes her. Throat parched, she downs two large glasses of water, fluffs up her pillows and sits up in her bed. She reviews her entire day, minute by minute, a day she's not about to forget. Something is nagging at her, she feels she's missing out on something essential, something decisive which evades her and that would show her the way. But what? The answer evades her. In the end, she gives up, takes a sleeping tablet and drops into a deep sleep.

*

Having parked her Mini nearby, Mary Lester walks towards the police station, slowly. The sedative has in fact worked far better than expected and she didn't hear her alarm ring. Amedeo will be delighted to catch her out. But she doesn't give a tinkers about Amedeo.

Of course, he is going to start with his innuendos about "agitated nights", "the things women do with their body" and Mary, although she hates doing it, will reply along the same lines because she knows it's the best way to annoy him: 'Well Monsieur, real men are so few and far between nowadays that when one finds a good lay, one has to make the most of it don't you think?'

After all, what does Amadeo care if Mary is late. He doesn't want her to do anything. The death of the tramp? Just drop it, Lester, an accident. Sallabert disappearing? Just a banal scarper, Lester, I'll take care of that. Interrogate the youths? You don't know how to go about it Lester, just leave that to the men.

So, what's left for Lester? Tell me boss, what's left?

'Well, you've got the statistics on juvenile delinquency during the first term, love. I'm sure you'll do a wonderful job. With plenty of percentages, and a nice graph with a curve. A downward curve, of course. Where delinquency is concerned Ministers love downward curves!'

Maybe. But Mary Lester doesn't like curves. She doesn't like paperwork. She doesn't like this police station that reeks of sweat, smelly feet and sour wine. This miserable stench makes her nauseated. She didn't join the police to become a secretary, otherwise she could have stayed with her lawyer. At least his offices were clean, even luxurious, the colleagues were polite and she wasn't spoken down to because she was a woman. Moreover, the pay was better.

So, Mary Lester, your training, the tough close combat sessions, the fast driving lessons, the firing range, all that was for nothing?

Well yes, for nothing. She must be a masochist, our little Mary, to have chosen this bloody job.

*

Sergeant Le Moal is leaving the station, yawning. He's been on night duty and has just finished. He's still wearing his uniform trousers and his black shoes but has left his cap and jacket in his locker. In this day and age, it's not always a good idea to take public transport wearing a copper's uniform.

He greets Mary.

'Bonjour Mademoiselle.'

'Bonjour Le Moal. Is Amedeo there?'

'No, he hasn't arrived yet.'

'Ah,' says Mary, relieved. 'Anything special happen last night Le Moal?'

'Nothing, Mademoiselle.'

'Are you going home?'

'Yes. I'm catching my bus.'

'I'll drive you home, Le Moal.'

Surprise cuts Le Moal's yawn midway. 'Sorry about that, it's the night duty. But Mademoiselle, you're embarrassing me, it's really too kind of you.'

'Don't worry, it won't take long. Do you know Kerhervy?'

'Do I know Kerhervy! In the summer I often go there with the wife and grandchildren. We take a picnic and play *boules*... Even in winter we go and practise there. There's a firing range in the quarry.'

'Do you shoot well, Le Moal?'

He laughs.

'Appallingly, Mademoiselle! With my gun I mean, because when I'm playing *boules*...'

They both laugh.

'That's not good for a copper,' says Mary mockingly frowning.

He laughs again. 'Come on, I don't need to be Buffalo Bill to man the reception and plug in telephone exchange leads.'

They both laugh again. Then Mary speaks more seriously.

'I'll tell you a secret, Le Moal. There's something I want to check out at Kerhervy and I'd like to be escorted by a man.'

'Oh! I see, its because of the gipsies I suppose.'

'The gipsies?' says Mary, puzzled. And then, she suddenly remembers that she *has* seen some caravans near a public rubbish dump. So she quickly adds: 'Yes, that's it, because of the gipsies.'

'It's not that they're much harm,' says Le Moal seriously, 'but, well, you never know with these people. Of course I'll go with you, Mademoiselle.'

CHAPTER V

Mary is driving fast. Next to her, Le Moal has somehow cramped himself into the passenger seat. The car is obviously not designed for fully-grown men and it's with relief that Le Moal extracts himself from the Mini when Mary parks by the outdoor theatre.

The scene hasn't changed. Embedded up to their bulwark rail, the old trawlers haven't budged an inch. Neither, apparently, have the cormorants. Mary feels comforted by the sergeant's presence. The cement patch is still there but somehow it has lost its malevolent power. It's just a plain old cement patch like you can find anywhere. The rain furrowed sand heap bears some obviously recent spade marks. There are also some deep tyre tracks in the waterlogged soil. Mary Lester pulls a tape-measure out of her pocket.

'Here, Le Moal, give me a hand. I'd like to measure the wheeltrack.'

'Ah?' says Le Moal, an image of perplexity.

'Put the tape in the middle of the tyre track. There… one metre fifty two. Fine. OK Le Moal, that's it then, we can go.'

'All right then, if that's all, we're off!'

The car bumps slowly along on the rutted reserve. Suddenly, Mary hits the brakes.

'What's that house, Le Moal?'

Overlooking the bay, hidden by a mass of brambles, stands an overgrown garden shed, painted pale green and as ugly as sin.

'That's Fanch Le Dantec's hut,' cries out Le Moal. 'Oh, what a story! Fifteen years ago, this hut was the talk of the town.'

Mary's inquisitive look invites him to carry on.

'Fanch Le Dantec was a workman at the Arsenal, a commie, a toughie, a shop steward. Fifteen years ago, he started building this hut without asking anyone's permission, more specifically without applying for a building permit, which of course would not have been granted given that the site is protected. In fact, it's precisely because the land couldn't be built on that Fanch Le Dantec got it so cheap. As expected, the authorities asked him to destroy the hut. Fortified by his position at the Arsenal, Fanch Le Dantec superbly ignored all summons. The authorities didn't give up but, rather craftily, Le Dantec brought the conflict out on familiar grounds: social conflicts. He delivered fiery speeches at the Arsenal: *If it had been some top knob who'd built a three-hundred-grand house there, no one would bother him. But when an honest workman builds a little hut with his own hands for his retirement, of course they want his guts for garters!* And the comrades from the union joined in the chorus: *Through our comrade Fanch Le Dantec, it's the entire union that's being attacked!* Well, the economic weight of the Arsenal is well known to all. As they say here: "when the Arsenal sneezes, it means the entire area is catching a cold"...'

'And so?'

'So, it went all the way up to the Ministry. The social climate wasn't exactly fantastic and small causes sometimes have great effects. Was a miserable hut really worth setting the entire area on fire? The Prefect's decision was final: wait and see.'

'So we're still waiting?'

'Yep. Le Dantec was due for retirement and everyone thought that, with his stepping out of the limelight, his impact would become negligible. It wouldn't take more than a year. We didn't even have to wait that long. Three years ago, on the 20th of November, Le Dantec was run over by a lorry and killed straight out whilst riding home from work on his moped'

'Wow, your memory's impressive!'

'Well, the merit's not that grand,' says the sergeant modestly. 'I was working that day and November 20th is my wife's name-day, *Sainte Marguerite's* day. We usually have a small celebration and, because of this accident, I got home late.'

'So, Le Dantec is dead,' says Mary Lester. 'And what became of the hut?'

'I don't know. The authorities haven't budged. And Le Dantec's pals are keeping a close eye on the whole affair. The hut has become a sort of symbol...'

'I see… If I read you properly, it's still here for a while.'

'Not sure. It's not very sturdy. And it's isolated. Madame Le Dantec has already lodged two or three complaints. The place's been broken into and vandalised. One day, a tree'll fall down on it and nobody will bother to repair it.'

Mary stops at the bottom of the path leading up to the hut and gets out of the car.

'Where are you going Mademoiselle?' asks Le Moal.

Mary nimbly jumps the rustic wooden fence and trots up the steep path. She turns around.

'I'm just going to have a look. The view must be great from up there.'

'I'll wait for you here if that's all right with you,' shouts Le Moal, not over keen on hill climbing.

The makeshift bungalow overlooks the sea. The windows are defended by thick wooden shutters, the massive door is neatly closed by a double security lock. In front of the doorway, the grass has been trampled. You can even see holes, like those made by high heeled shoes, women's shoes. The lock has also been oiled recently and the overflow has dribbled down the wood panel, leaving a shiny oily streak.

That's all. After admiring the view, which is indeed remarkable, Mary Lester returns to her car.

'The view is superb up there,' she says to Le Moal. 'Despite its ugliness, the house must be quite pleasant in summer. Do you know if anybody comes here any more?'

'I don't know,' says Le Moal. 'Madame Le Dantec doesn't drive and walks with difficulty… and two walking sticks. She's got arthritis in the hips or something like that. The poor woman probably couldn't even make it to the pathway, let alone climb up it. Anyhow, I think she's in a nursing home now.'

The little car is travelling towards Lanester.

'Where do you live, Le Moal?'

'Oh, don't worry about me. Just drop me at the first bus stop, Mademoiselle.'

'Of course not. I'm driving you home. I've wasted enough of your time as it is. Unless you're worried your wife might get jealous if she sees you in the car with me?'

Le Moal laughs.

'Oh no, she won't mind.'

'I have something to ask you Le Moal, and that's to keep our little drive to yourself. Amedeo's really got it in for me these days and he's quite capable of finding something wrong with our little jaunt.'

'Don't worry, Mademoiselle, you can count on me. Anyhow, I've been off duty for the past hour which means I'm free to go where I want with who I want.'

*

Mary Lester drops Le Moal off just a couple of yards from his house. The fat man has completely forgotten how tired he was and is obviously delighted by his little outing with the trainee detective constable. Mary then makes for the nursing home.

Like all geriatric dumps, the place exudes sadness. You can feel death prowling along the grim corridors where greenish yellow paint is flaking away behind overheated radiators. A procession of bleary eyed little old ladies, some desperately gripping their Zimmer frames, others clutching their faded out dressing gowns tightly around long forgotten busts, is slowly progressing under the supervision of an overworked would-be cheerful auxiliary.

Madame Le Dantec is in her room. She sits herself on the edge of her bed to leave the room's only chair to her visitor.

'So, you're in the police?'

'Yes Madame Le Dantec.'

'I thought you were a social worker at first. Is this about the Kerhervy house again?'

'Yes. How did you know?'

'It's not difficult' answers the old lady with a faint smile. 'That house is nothing but trouble.'

'I'm not here to cause trouble, Madame Le Dantec,' says Mary Lester in what she hopes is an engaging tone.

Madame Le Dantec pulls a sceptical face. 'Oh no? What for then?' She obviously doesn't trust Mary. For her, like for most people, the word "police" can only spell trouble. Never mind whether it comes from a charming young woman or a coarse pot-bellied constable.

'I would just like some information.'

'Ah? About Kerhervy?'

'Yes.'

The walls are decorated with prints and photos from merrier times. From his gilt-edged frame, a stout man with a moustache is looking down disapprovingly at Mary. With his cap set at an angle, his dark scarf around his neck, his hairy forearms crossed on his chest, his hard stare and not the shadow of a smile on his face, the man certainly doesn't look easy going. Mary presumes that this is the late Fanch Le Dantec, the hard-line shop steward.

'Is that your husband?'

Frowning over her tortoise shell glasses, the old lady follows Mary's gaze.

'Yes.' Then, after a moment of silence, she continues in her faint voice: 'From the day he brought that bit of land, we never had a moment's peace. He knew very well building wasn't allowed out there, but there was no point in telling him. He wasn't an easy man to get along with. And stubborn with it!… Oh well… he's dead now…'

Mary turns back towards Le Dantec's widow. Her life must have been quite remote from the proverbial bowl of cherries.

'And,' she adds, 'I didn't like it out there.' She points towards her two walking sticks leaning against the bed. 'You've seen the house. How do you expect me to go up that goat track with these?'

On the bedside table, in a small gilt frame, the photo of two little boys.

'Are these you grandchildren?'

The old lady leans over and smiles tenderly to the photo.

'Yes Mademoiselle.'
'And do they like Kerhervy?'
'They never go there. Their fathers, my sons, work in the Paris area.'
'Well surely, you see them for the holidays don't you?'
'No. They say there's not enough sunshine out here. They go to Spain with their caravan. Since their father's funeral, they've never been back.'
There is a pathetic resignation in her voice.
'And what's happened to this blasted house now?'
'Nothing, don't worry,' says Mary. She pulls Antoine Sallabert's photo out of her bag.
'Do you know this man?'
Madame Le Dantec adjusts her glasses, which had slipped down the bridge of her nose, looks attentively at the photo and smiles faintly.
'Yes, well, I mean I've already seen him. I don't know his name. He came to see me about six months ago. The house at Kerhervy had just been burgled. The shutters had been broken and there was quite a bit of damage. They even spoke of it in the press. I didn't know what to do with the house. I can't look after it and it's not sellable. This man came to see me and asked if he could rent it. He said he'd take care of the repairs and that I wouldn't have to do anything. He gave me five hundred francs and I gave him the keys. That's all.'
'That's all' echoes Mary.
'Yes. Every thirtieth, I find an envelope in my letter box with a five hundred franc note in it.'

Her voice takes on an imploring tone as she grasps Mary's wrist. 'Tell me, Mademoiselle, am I going to be in trouble?'

'Of course not,' says Mary. 'Why should we...'

'But if the police are looking for this man... What has he done?'

'He's disappeared, Madame Le Dantec.'

The old lady had been expecting everything but that.

'Disappeared?' Disappeared from Kerhervy?'

'We don't know for sure yet,' says Mary. 'His wife reported his disappearance yesterday. The usual investigation is under way. Would you by any chance have another set of keys to the house?'

'Yes, somewhere around here.' She rummages in her bedside table and hands Mary a flat key.

'Do I have your permission to visit the house?'

'Of course.'

'Thank you Madame Le Dantec. I'll check the house out and return your key as soon as possible.'

Madame Le Dantec shrugs her skinny shoulders.

'Oh, there's no rush, you know.'

Mary stands up.

'Au revoir Madame Le Dantec.'

The old lady leans forwards, pushing on the bed with her fists as if trying to get up. Mary makes an appeasing gesture. 'Please don't bother.'

She leaves, gently closing the door behind her.

*

The house at Kerhervy contains a large single room, definitely cosier than what one might have feared judging by its outside appearance. The walls and ceiling are panelled in sand colour pine, not unlike a boat cabin. On the floor, the coldness of the dark red hexagonal waxed tiles is mitigated by a large white woollen carpet. Mary's inspection doesn't take long: a double bed, a tiny kitchen corner, a table covered with a yellow oilcloth, a chimney dominated by a large riveted sheet metal hood with a stack of dry wood next to it.

The shop steward's pals probably gave him a hand to decorate his country house. The Arsenal counts excellent workmen of all trades.

The bed is made. The place quite clean. On the table, a large size box of matches is conveniently sitting next to a thick six-branch copper chandelier holding half burnt candles. Near the sink, a low voltage lamp bulb is powered by a car battery.

A right little love nest, thinks Mary. All I need to know now is who our randy friend shared it with, and that's not going to be easy. The CenterMarket staff includes roughly one hundred employees, not counting the women who come round every day asking for a job. Did the manager take advantage of this plentiful source? Was he one of those bosses who use their position to seduce women? Did he have a regular or did he only use this place for one-night stands?

So many questions, unanswered for the time being.

Mary leaves; the door closes soundlessly behind her. Like the lock, the hinges have been carefully oiled. It's nice outside. People are even taking a stroll. This time, Mary has no apprehension at the idea of returning alone to Kerhervy. Lost in thought, she climbs back in her car. Off we go to the Lorient police station. Off we go towards statistics and falling curves.

*

To hell with statistics, they'll just have to wait! Mechanically, Mary grabs a piece of paper and starts writing:

- One dead drowned tramp;
- One vanished manager;
- One stolen van, now a wreck;
- One burgled country house;
- One patch of cement by the waterside;
- One drum? print in the stolen van;
- Tyre prints in Kerhervy;
- One discreet love nest for the vanished manager;
- One bridge over the Scorff without guardrail;
- One blockhouse.

Mary sighs. What an inventory! What can the link be between all these elements?

The tramp, the railway bridge without guardrail, the blockhouse, the bed-base, the gas cooker, the drum. All in the same neighbourhood. The tramp lived under the bridge, from which he supposedly fell. The bedbase, the gas cooker, the drum are in the mud under the bridge. The place isn't exactly wanting for rubbish.

The vanished manager had a secluded love nest in Kerhervy.

The youths found the manager's van on the Kerhervy road.

The van was used to transport cement, like in Kerhervy, and maybe a drum, like the one under the railway bridge. The wheel prints near the cement patch in Kerhervy are similar to the van's.

No matter what, she always ends up in the same spots: the railway bridge and Kerhervy, Kerhervy and the railway bridge…

Why is there a drum under the railway bridge?

Mary jumps up and runs along the corridor, bumping into detective constable Berger on her way. He's nice, is Berger. Mary liked him straight away.

He belongs to the new generation of policemen, more relaxed, less imbued with their prerogatives. What a pity the Chief Superintendent hasn't given her Berger for boss. Things would have been so much easier.

'Hey Mary,' says Berger, 'what's the big hurry? You catching a train or something?' This is Berger's usual way of speaking and Mary is not offended. Ensconced in her investigation, she grabs him by the elbow. 'Tell me, Berger, why is there a drum under the railway bridge?'

'A what?' asks a bemused Berger.

'A drum,' says Mary, 'a large metal cylinder, if you prefer.'

Berger laughs.

'I don't prefer, thank you very much. But why shouldn't there be a drum under the railway bridge? There's old drums everywhere. Milk churns, oil drums, oil cans, there's cans all over the place these days. Even here, we keep putting people in the can.'

Mary shakes his arm.

'Come off it Berger, this is serious!'

'Ah! it's serious. Oh well, that changes everything then.' exclaims Berger emphatically. 'You should ask a serious person then, not that you'll find that many here.' He mimics intense reflection, chin on his right hand and left hand to his brow. 'You're in luck though, I know one sitting right next door. Follow me.'

He leads Mary to the switchboard where Le Moal has resumed his crosswording activities.

'There's the man you need. Tell us, Le Moal, you who know everything, tell us why is there a drum under the railway bridge?'

Le Moal frowns, as bemused as Berger was earlier on.

'A drum?'

'Yes,' says Berger, 'a drum, a large drum, an enormous drum!'

Le Moal's bewildered gaze travels from Mary to Berger and from Berger to Mary. He opts for a large grin. 'Oh come on Berger, you're pulling my leg. What's this bullshit?'

'Ask Mary. She's worried. She's spotted a large drum under the railway bridge.'

'In the channel?' asks Le Moal.

'Not quite,' says Mary. 'In the mud, not far from the shore.'

'Oh, then it'll be a mooring, Mademoiselle,' says Le Moal with the quiet conviction of the knowledgeable.

Mary frowns.

'A mooring?'

'Yes, a mooring to moor boats to. Out here, the guys just fill an old tyre or an old drum with cement to make a sturdy mooring. It has to be pretty hefty as the current can get really strong with the spring tides.'

'But this one,' says Mary disconcerted by the obvious simplicity of her question, 'this one doesn't have a boat tied to it.'

'It's probably gone out to sea, or else it's been taken out of the water for the winter.'

'Ah,' says Mary in a very faint voice.

Berger is laughing his head off.

'Well there, little Mary, you see, it was quite simple. It was just a case of asking the right person. Thank you Le Moal for giving us the benefit of your wisdom.'

Le Moal chuckles in turn. Honestly, what these women won't split hairs about.

Not really convinced, Mary leaves with Berger who's still roaring his head off.

'Stop laughing, you great idiot!' she says, mad.

Berger comes to a halt in the middle of the corridor and, emphatic: 'After questioning, insults! Mademoiselle, I won't allow you…'

Mary grabs him by the lapels and shakes him.

'Berger…'

Berger mimics Amedeo: 'Now what, love?'

Mary stamps her feet with impatience.

'Oh cut it out Berger! I want this drum brought out.'

'Is that all,' says Berger. 'And so?'

'How do I go about it?'

Berger puts on a great show of make-believe brain racking. 'Now then, let's see. First you need a heavy-duty fishing line mounted with a large hook and baited with… I don't know… an oil-soaked rag maybe?… You cast it near the drum and wait for it to rise.'

Furious, Mary kicks him in the shins: 'You dope!'

'Ouch!' cries out Berger, hopping ostentatiously around on one leg. His war dance completed, he sobers down and asks earnestly: 'What's this drum done to you?'

'I don't know. It's fishy!'

Berger solemnly nods his head: 'You've found a fishy drum.'

'Yes' cries out Mary with conviction.

'Well,' guffaws Berger, 'I guess a fishy drum makes a nice change of suspect.' Very pleased with himself, he creases up again.

Infuriated, Mary shrugs her shoulders.

'For Christ's sake, Berger, will you stop farting around! This is serious.'

'No it isn't little Mary,' says Berger, speaking to Mary as to a child. 'The river's full of drums, Le Moal's just told you so. What's suspicious about that?'

'I did tell you, Berger, that my drum was just under the bridge didn't I?'

'Sure you did. Rather twice than once.'

'Well, on the shore, there's this huge board. And do you know what's written on this board in bold red and black letters, you mule?'

'Mule yourself! No, I don't know what's written in bold red and black letters on your bloody board and, what's more, I don't give a damn!'

'Yes, obviously you don't' says Mary, tears welling. 'You guys really are bastards! There's no point in asking you to give a hand.'

Berger suddenly realises that he's been a bit too harsh with little Mary whom he rather likes. In a gentler tone, he asks: 'OK then. Tell me what is written in bold red and black letters on your large board.'

Mary sniffles and complies.

'It says: *High voltage cables. Distance: 7 metres downstream from the bridge. No anchoring or mooring within 20 metres.*'

'I don't see…' says Berger.

'Do you really think someone would drop his mooring where it's forbidden, just opposite the Arsenal? Do you really think a boat is moored just under the bridge? The coastguards would have it moved in a jiffy.'

'Yeees,' says Berger, not convinced. 'You might have something there. But, well, I don't see what we can do about it. You ought to speak to Amedeo about it. After all, he is your mentor isn't he?'

Mary storms back to her office, furious. Speak to Amedeo about it! Thank you Berger. Amedeo's certainly the last person she wants to talk to. She must absolutely get that drum fished out. But how? And that van, was it driven to Kerhervy on Monday night?

CHAPTER VI

By now, Mary knows the Kerhervy road by heart. Not far from the main road, yet another housing estate is under construction. Much further inland, an isolated farm, with gipsies for nearest neighbours.

On a muddy strip of land four caravans surrounded by detritus are parked. A measly fire is dying away, a picketed miniature goat is bleating pitifully, some non too clean laundry is trying to dry on a sagging line.

Not a cheerful setting. The caravans, however, are brand new, the cars pricey Mercedes.

Mary stops and gets out of her car. A mangy underfed dog crawls out from beneath one of the caravans and starts howling dolefully, obviously prepared to dart back between the wheels at the least sign of danger.

A curtain is pulled, a door opens.

'Yes, what is it?'

Two none too friendly black eyes glare at Mary. A dirty young woman steps out, accompanied by a whiff of stale air. She's holding a baby in one arm and a snotty-nosed toddler is clinging to her skirts.

'I'd like some information'.

'Information?' repeats the woman suspiciously.

'Have you been here long?'

'What's it to you? Is it forbidden to park here? There's no sign to say so.'

You bet there isn't, thinks Mary, you pulled it out when you arrived! Then she realises that this isn't going to be easy.

The woman continues, increasingly hostile: 'I know. They've set us up a new campsite, just next to the highway. Are you from the town hall?' And, without waiting for Mary's answer: 'Well you can tell them people at the Town hall that they can shove their campsite! We've always camped here and we've no intention of changing. That fucking campsite of theirs is surrounded with wire netting. It's like a prison. And, on top of that, there's no way you can sleep out there for the noise from the motorway.'

'There are cars that go by here too,' offers Mary.

'One every now and then. Nothing like out there where it's a non stop flow of traffic, day and night. And then you've got the lorries changing gears at the roundabout...'

'Can you tell me if you heard any cars driving by on Monday night?'

'What for?'

'I work for an insurance company,' asserts Mary confidently. 'I need to know whether a van drove along this road on Monday night.'

'And why should I tell you?'

'For the reward, for instance.'

'The reward?' says the woman, frowning.

'Oh, it's only a small reward, for a small piece of information.'

And, as the woman isn't answering, she pulls a two-hundred franc note out of her pocket and shows it to her.

'So?'

The woman eyes the offering suspiciously, wondering where the catch lays.

'Every Monday evening,' she says reluctantly, 'there's a van goes by at about five or six o'clock. It's the CenterMarket van. It's written on it. We've been wondering what it was doing, seeing that nobody else lives out here.'

'Does it stay long?'

'It usually leaves at about eight.'

'And what about last Monday?'

'It was different. I heard the van leave as usual but it came back and left again around midnight.'

'Are you sure?'

'Certain. I saw it like I see you. The baby's teething, you see, so I'm woken up at all hours.'

The words are gushing between her thin lips and her strange accent makes her difficult to understand. Her dark eyes are riveted to the note that Mary holds firmly.

'So, you saw the van leave around midnight.'

'That's what I've just told you, isn't it' says the woman impatiently, 'you can hear the cars climbing the hill long before they're here. I pulled the curtain aside mechanically and saw it go by.'

'Was it going back to Lanester?'

'Yes.'

'Tell me, Madame, when the van arrives around six, isn't there another car that goes by just about at the same time?'

'Yes, a Peugeot 205 convertible.'
'Ah!... And do they also leave at the same time?'
'Yes, they follow each other pretty closely.'
'And this hasn't intrigued you?'
The woman shrugs her shoulders, resettling the baby against her left shoulder at the same time. The toddler is still clinging to her rags, sucking its snotty fingers with delight.
'Pfff! probably lovers going to the woods for a bit of fun 'n' games. In summer, there's a lot of them, but they must be pretty desperate to mess around outside in this season!'
'And on Monday night, they didn't leave together?'
'No, the white car left at about eight o'clock as usual.'
'And at what time did the van leave?'
Once again, the gipsy shrugs her shoulders.
'Not long after. Half an hour maybe. I don't know.'
'Weren't you surprised to see it return later?' asks Mary.
'What's it to me! It's a free country!'
'At what time did you see it come back?'
'Around half past nine. I didn't see it, I heard it. I recognised the noise of the engine. And when it went away again, it was even noisier. It was having a hard job going up the hill.'
Mary hands the note to the woman who snatches it without a word of thanks. More politely, Mary says:
'Well, thank you very much, Madame.'
The gipsy watches her walk away. Her distrust hasn't diminished a bit. She'll never understand these gadjés[Tr. Note] who fork out good money just to meddle in other people's affairs.

Tr. Note : "Gadjo" *(pl.* gadjés*) is the name French-speaking gipsies give to people who are not gipsies.*

Mary climbs back into her car and rushes back to Lanester. By God, it might have cost her two hundred francs, but talk about return on investment!

*

Back at the station, Amedeo corners her.

'So Lester, I've heard you want to fish out all the old drums floating on the Scorff and the Blavet? You should've joined the antipollution squad, love, not the police. Come on, Lester, come back to earth will you. I'm not against a laugh, but you're pushing things a bit far. The entire station has been laughing at your latest quirk all afternoon.'

Mary glares back at him, thinking: *Quirk? I'll give you quirks!*

Amedeo reads her thoughts.

'And there's no need to glare at me like that. You know damn well I'm right. For Christ's sakes, what do they teach you at police school? Tomorrow, you're going back to Lanester, right.'

'Yes Monsieur,' says Mary. Her mind is bubbling: Lanester! Again! Glued to a chair all day listening to country bumpkins complaining that they've had three cabbage heads stolen. What a job!

*

The only distinctive feature of the otherwise quite ordinary Lanester police station door is a plain brass plate stating: *Please ring once and come in.*

Aimable Maugracieux dutifully rings, enters, and, spotting Mary, stops dead.

'Oh... It's you!' he exclaims.

'It's me,' says Mary. 'Bonjour Monsieur Maugracieux.'

'It's you who... It's you that...' mumbles an embarrassed Aimable.

'Yes Monsieur Maugracieux, it's me who's on duty. What can I do for you?'

'My boat's been stolen,' says Aimable, indignant.

'Oh, where from?'

'From the log dock, where I... where we found...'

'Where you found the body of Maurice Toussaint?'

'Precisely!'

'Was it moored properly?'

'You bet it was! With a galvanised chain, two turns around the stem and a brass padlock. I goes out there this morning...'

'To pick winkles?' asks Mary perfidiously.

'No, I've gone off winkles, thank you very much' says Aimable pulling a disgusted face. 'No, I went to check that the boat hadn't drifted with the spring tide. And when I got there, no boat! Someone's stolen her.'

'Is the mooring still in place?'

'Of course it is. There's no way that's going to budge. It's an old tyre filled with cement. Weighs at least one hundred kilos. Someone's nicked her I tell you. The chain's been cut with a bolt cutter.'

'Are you sure?'

'Sure, I'm sure, look, I even found the missing link.'

He places the neatly cut half-link in front of Mary.

'Have you looked upstream? Downstream?'

'I walked down to the railway bridge and then all the way up to Pont Saint-Christophe, but she wasn't there. She could have got quite far. If she's been let loose when the tide was coming in, she's probably in Pont-Scorff by now and in the opposite case, she'll be somewhere between Larmor and Port-Louis. This country's really going to pot. We've become a nation of thieves!'

Mary grabs a sheet of paper.

'And what does you boat look like, Monsieur Maugracieux?'

'She's black with a red molding. She's a four metres sixty flat-bottomed boat and she's called "*Angèle*".'

'Does she have an engine?'

'Not when I'm away. It's an outboard and I bring it home with me each time.'

Mary notes, repeating out loud: 'One small black and red boat without engine...'

Vaguely vexed, Maugracieux comments: 'Small... small... she's not that small! She's big enough to go fishing with. And even if she's no yacht, that's no reason to steal her.'

Mary looks up at the plaintiff and says sternly: 'Nobody's saying that Monsieur.'

'No,' says Maugracieux bitterly, 'you did not say it. But Maugracieux is no fool. He knows. You don't give a tinker's about my boat. You don't give a damn because she's not worth millions. You couldn't care less. These days, nobody gives a damn about anything in this rotten country. Same as you're pretending to register my complaint, but I know that, as soon as I'll have turned around, that sheet of paper'll go straight in the bin.'

Mary raises her voice. The man is beginning to get on her nerves.

'Please, Monsieur Maugracieux, let's be serious!'

'There you are,' says Maugracieux raising his arms to heaven, 'it's me that's not serious now. Of course! I'm the one who's robbed and on top of that I get insulted. What next?'

Maugracieux' insincerity is such that, beyond her exasperation, Mary is beginning to have fun.

'Just a minute, Monsieur Maugracieux, who's insulting you?'

'Well, you said I wasn't serious. Did I hear wrong? Next thing, you're going to think that I'm deaf, subject to hallucinations and pissed out of my mind. Me, not serious? Watch it, Mademoiselle, you mind what you say!'

Mary can't believe her ears. Caught between a rising giggle and a strong desire to give the man an earful, she just nods at Maugracieux.

Maugracieux leans over towards her.

'Now you listen to me, young lady, even if you are a detective constable, I'll tell you something else: if I had my word in it, thieves would have their right hand chopped off when first caught. And the left when caught at it again.'

Mary only just manages to keep a straight face.

'Why, what you're saying is quite clever Monsieur Maugracieux. I'm sure this method would seriously cut down the rate of third attempts.'

'Ah! You see.' says Maugracieux triumphantly, 'you see, I'm not that silly.'

'Such a simple and cost-effective measure,' says Mary, by now having a very hard time refraining her giggles. 'And to think nobody's suggested it yet.'

'Oh,' says Maugracieux cunningly, 'it's not that no one's ever thought of it. I'll tell you something: pardon my French, but our government has no balls. MPs, senators, ministers and all that lot, a bunch of layabouts sitting pretty in their cosy seats. But as far as responsibility is concerned, zilch, zero, there's nobody home! So, bicycles get stolen, boats get stolen, padlocks get cut…'

Mary cuts the inventory short.

'Were the oars aboard?'

'Well, yes, I'm not going to cart'em home with me every time, am I.'

Mary stands up.

'Right, Monsieur Maugracieux. I'll send a word out about your boat's disappearance. On your side, do you think you could check the riverside just in case she's grounded somewhere?'

'The shame of it,' cries out Maugracieux, 'you can't own anything these days. And on top of that, it's me who has to look for her! What's this country come to?' He briefly salutes Mary and grumbles his way out.

Mary smiles. Poor Maugracieux. This just isn't his lucky week. Yesterday he finds a stiff and today he looses his boat. He'll end up moving to some remote haven in the countryside, that's for sure.

CHAPTER VII

The door opens and reveals a sixtyish gentleman wearing a dark suit with the little red dot of the *Légion d'Honneur* on the lapel. Startled, Mary looks up.

'Chief Superintendent!' she cries, jumping up.

'Hello Mademoiselle Lester, did I startle you?'

Chief Superintendent Lucien Fabien is a legend in the police: impeccably dressed, elegant, always courteous, never trivial, he is highly respected by all.

'Not really,' mumbles Mary. 'I'm afraid I was daydreaming Monsieur. But then, I wasn't expecting you.'

'You were dreaming of drums maybe?'

Mary blushes.

'Oh, Monsieur, you were told?'

The super laughs benignly.

'Well I am supposed to know what's happening in my services, detective constable Lester. What are things like here this morning?'

'Not much to say, really,' says Mary grabbing the daybook.

'Some kids have broken Madame Adrienne Thibaut's window panes with their catapults. Two rabbits were stolen from Monsieur Anselme Martin's rabbit hutch in full daylight while he was taking his afternoon nap, and Monsieur Aimable Maugracieux's boat has disappeared.'

The Chief Super sits down and sighs.

'Not exactly thrilling, is it Lester?'

He's smiling. Mary smiles back.

'That's the least one can say, Monsieur.'

'And that's not what you expected when you joined the police force, is it?'

'Well, no, not exactly Monsieur.'

'So, you're rather disappointed.'

Mary shrugs her shoulders.

'A bit.'

The Chief Superintendent stretches out his legs and carefully rearranges the impeccable crease of his trousers.

'Ah, Mary Lester, you're impatient… Here, I'll tell you a story: in 1944, I was sixteen when I joined the army. I was rearing to go and fight, my dreams were full of clandestine air drops and lurking snipers… Do you know what I did throughout the entire war?'

'No Monsieur.'

'I peeled spuds in the stinking kitchen of a sordid canteen. I peeled spuds from morning to evening. I peeled so many spuds that the sight of a plain chip is enough to make me feel sick even now.'

'And after that, Monsieur?'

'After that I was demobbed. I went back to school, took law and joined the police, like you.

And, like you, I had to prove myself. Like you, I filled in endless complaint books in remote police stations which were often much less pleasant than this one. Broken letter boxes, "borrowed" mopeds, vanishing car radios, disappearing rabbits…'

He smiles.

'You're probably wondering why on earth I'm telling you all this? It's to make you understand that you've got to prove yourself Lester. As my grandfather used to say —he was an old-time sailor who rounded Cape Horn several times—, you've got to be a seaman before you can be captain. All in good time, Lester. You'll see, things will get moving much sooner than you think so.'

He stands up.

'Like you, I started in a small local station, in Roubaix. It feels like that was just yesterday and to think I'm due for retirement in only two months time. You'll see, Lester, life flies by so quickly that before you've got time to say Jack Robinson, you're halfway through it. Come on then, let's go and see that drum of yours.'

Mary doesn't need to be told twice.

'But, what if Monsieur Amedeo asks for me?'

The superintendent smiles again.

Monsieur Amedeo isn't going to ask for you. Monsieur Amedeo is in bed with a nasty cold. A cold as nasty as sudden, I must say.

*

The Chief Superintendent drives his own Peugeot 405 at a leisurely pace. The car reflects the man: impeccable, both outside and in. They reach the log dock. The tide has pulled out and only a thin trickle of water is meandering through the glittering black mud.

'So, where is this famous drum?' asks the Chief Superintendent.

'Under the bridge, out there' says Mary pointing towards the metal structure barring the horizon.

The car slows down and stops. The air is rich with low-tide smells. In the distance, metallic noises can be heard from behind the Arsenal wall, a forbidding breeze-block job topped with barbed wire. Far away downstream a tug moos three times.

The Chief Superintendent takes a few steps on the yellow grass verge and looks around. The bridge is still under repair and herring gulls are loudly fighting over a prey in what remains of the channel.

'But,' he says, 'there's a boat moored to that drum of yours Lester.'

'Ah,' says Mary disconcerted. 'It wasn't there yesterday.'

'It looks like you made a mountain out of a molehill, love.'

And now he's calling me love too, thinks Mary bitterly.

The Chief Superintendent continues:

'It wasn't there yesterday and today it is. Boats come and go…'

'But… it's *Angèle*!' shouts out Mary.

'*Angèle*?' repeats the Chief Superintendent, frowning.

'Yes,' says Mary who, by now, has completely recovered from her bout of depression. '*Angèle*. The boat stolen from Aimable Maugracieux! He came to lodge a complaint this morning. Strange though that he didn't see it given that it's just under the bridge, only three hundred metres from it's usual mooring… He did say he had looked here…'

She looks interrogatingly at the superintendent who looks back at her, amused.

'I know,' she says, 'the tide was high this morning.'

'Yees, and it was low at midday' says the Superintendent, not without a trace of irony in his voice.

'So, if Maugracieux couldn't see his boat, it's because it had sunk.'

Fabien frowns.

'What do you mean, sunk? Listen Lester, I am finding you a little difficult to follow.'

Mary turns round towards him as if she hadn't heard.

'Chief, we must absolutely fish that drum out.'

Fabien shakes his head, apparently giving up all hopes of ever bringing this kid back to reason.

'But why, Lester, why?'

'Because someone's tried to move it, chief,' she says excitedly, now desperate for her boss to share her convictions. 'There's a guy who has chucked this drum here with God knows what inside it. He must've seen me nosing around several times. He got scared because he has a damn good reason for not wanting that drum fished out. So, he takes advantage of the spring tide and steals the nearest boat. At mid-tide, he rows near the drum, moors the boat to it, but very short, and waits for the tide to come in. The tide should lift both the boat and the drum. After that, all he has to do is let the outgoing tide carry him downstream and, when he's far enough in the middle of the channel, where there's always water, he cuts the rope. His idea is that the drum disappears and Mary Lester's going to looks a right fool when she comes for it. But…'

'But,' completes the superintendent who's as sharp as they come, 'the drum was too heavy, the boat wasn't able to lift it and so it sunk.'

'That's it boss! Do you see now why we must absolutely fish that drum out!'

CHAPTER VIII

'You're lucky the chief fireman is a friend of mine,' says Chief Superintendent Fabien sitting behind the small reception desk of the Lanester police station.

He grabs the phone and, sighing once again, dials the number.

'Hello, the fire brigade? I'd like to speak to Captain Laurent please... Chief Superintendent Fabien.'

Covering the phone with his hand, he says to Lester who's sitting in front of him: 'This will save us a good bit of form-filling and...'

Mary will never know the end of the sentence as he suddenly takes his hand away from the receiver and says:

'Hello, is that you Laurent? Yes, Fabien speaking... Why I'm calling? Well, as usual, I've got a favour to ask from you. No, nothing serious... Routine really. One of my detective constables has spotted a suspicious drum under the railway bridge... Explosives? No, certainly not. But we're in the middle of a delicate affair, a missing person case, and this drum might contain interesting evidence. Nothing certain mind you, but, you know, we can't overlook anything… That's it. I'd like you to fish that drum out discreetly. You can? This afternoon? Wonderful! I'll send you my detective constable right away. Thanks again Laurent.'

He hangs up.

'Well, there you are young lady. I hope you're satisfied. All you have to do now is go to the fire brigade and ask for Captain Laurent. He'll do whatever's needed to fish out your drum.'

Mary is overjoyed.

'Oh, thank you boss!'

As she's dashing out, Fabien stops her.

'Lester, I want you to phone me as soon as that drum is out of the water. Tell the firemen to store it in their garage and do nothing else until I'm there. And, Lester, discretion is our motto! I don't want a word out to the press before we know where we stand.'

Mary thinks that what the Chief Superintendent is really worried about is looking a fool but she couldn't care less, the drum's going to be fished out and that's all she sees.

Her arrival at the fire brigade does not go unnoticed. Instead of the expected detective constable, this rather dishy young woman turns up. But Mary ignores the leery looks and ironical grins, she loves these firemen who are going to fish out her bloody drum and she's prepared to forgive them anything.

She worries about how they're going to go about it. The chief of the expedition, a tall blond guy with blue eyes, smiles.'Fish out a drum? Child's play!' He explains the procedure to Mary: first of all, deploy a robust net on the mud, then roll the drum onto it, close the net so as to capture it. After that, tie a buoy to the lot, inflate the buoy with compressed air from the bottle sitting in the inflatable dinghy and wait for the tide to come in.

Child's play…'

The whole operation is roundly conducted. Then, they start waiting —unbearable for Mary— but tides can't be rushed and this one won't be full before six o'clock. Nothing doing till then. The firemen wait in their van, smoking a cigarette. Now and then their radio spits out a bit of news, a call. Mary sits in her little car and listens to Mozart's requiem. The chief fireman has told her that she could go and catch a bite to eat but nothing doing. She's staying. Wild horses wouldn't drag her away from that drum.

Every now and then she gets out of her car and checks on what's happening. Intrigued by the red van parked by the river, some passers-by stop to inquire. The tall blond man tells them it's an exercise, that they're trying out new equipment to recover wrecks. Their curiosity satisfied, the onlookers leave, nodding their heads with approval for such conscientious professionals.

At last, the water licks the wheels of the trailer. The dinghy slides smoothly on its rollers into the water, the powerful outboard roars into life and they make for the big red buoy to which they attach a sturdy hawser for the towing.

The fifty-five horsepower engine roars, spitting out blue fumes on the water surface. At first, the dinghy rears up but soon settles and they slowly make for the shore. A sudden shock, boat and buoy stop dead. They're still far from the shore.

'What *are* they up to?' asks Mary now frantic with impatience.

'There's not enough water' peacefully answers the tall blond. We'll have to wait a little longer.'

'Wait, wait, wait! All we ever do is wait.'

'There's no point getting your knickers in a twist' says the phlegmatic fireman, 'There's nothing else we can do. Your drum's well and truly secured now, it's not going to run away.'

Mary shrugs her shoulders. Oh yes, very clever! She knows damn well it's not going to run away. But of course, this fireman doesn't care. He's been asked to fish out a drum, he fishes the drum out, period. He's doing it rather well, in fact. Nothing to report. But he's not worried about the drum's contents. What's it to him if it's just full of cement, like everyone thinks it is? But for her, Mary… Oh God! She daren't even think of it. She's both scared that it may be empty and scared of what might be in it.

If it's empty, she hasn't finished hearing about it. She might as well apply for her transfer straight away. And even then, Amedeo's bound to find a way of passing the word on to wherever she might be posted.

If the drum contains what she thinks it does, it's not going to be a pretty sight.

The fireman comes back to her.

'And what is it you're hoping to find in there by the way? Drugs, jewels, counterfeit money?' he asks with a quietly ironic smile.

'A body,' says Mary stiffly.

'Is that all?'

'That's all.'

The fireman looks at her differently now.

'Are you serious?'

Mary smiles at him. He's rather nice this guy, but he can't understand. She speaks more gently.

'What do you think? That this is my idea of fun?'

'Blow me!' says the fireman.

The tide is full now, it's nearly reaching the road. The dinghy lands, the firemen jump ashore and moor it to the crash barrier.

The weather is mild. Not a whiff of wind. The calm water mirrors the luminous grey of the sky. Further down, beyond the bridge, a Navy tug is moving some barges around.

The firemen haul on the rope vigorously and the drum emerges, wrapped in the net.

'Louis, tie this to the tow bar,' says the tall blond. 'There's no point in wrecking our backs, we'll pull it out with the van.'

With a roar of the engine, the Peugeot van extracts the load.

'OK,' says Louis to the tall blond who's driving. 'Dédé, get the planks out.'

Dédé, a small thickset man built like a tank opens the back of the van, takes out two pine planks and positions them to form a ramp. He removes the net from the drum.

'Ok guys, let's get it in'.

All together, they roll the drum up the ramp.

'Heave ho!' One last shove and that's it, the drum is in the van.

'Well done!' says Mary full of admiration. 'I thought you'd never make it. That thing must weigh a ton.'

'More like three hundred kilos' says the tall blond. 'Hey, Dédé, I hope you've wedged it properly. I don't want that thing rolling around in the van.'

'Not to worry,' says Dédé, 'it won't budge. And anyhow, we're not going to drive as if we were going to put out a fire.'

'I'll meet you at the fire-station,' says Mary. 'I've got to phone my boss but please remember we have to be as discreet as possible.'

'No problem,' says the tall blond. 'We'll store the drum in the garage and wait for your boss to arrive. See you later.'

As dusk is falling, Mary drives off in her Mini.

*

She's waiting in the fire station yard. Night has fallen. Part of the courtyard is lit up by one of the street lampposts. In the main building, a few windows are lit up and a radio is playing in the distance. In the ground floor office, like all his colleagues worldwide, the on-duty officer is doing the crosswords and yawning.

The firemen have stored the drum in their workshop before parking the dinghy and its trailer in another garage.

Mary paces the yard, consumed with impatience and anxiety. The Chief Superintendent said he was coming straight away. Something must've kept him.

Each time headlights appear through the gate,

Mary jumps up. At last, a car shows up at the courtyard entrance. The electric gate rises. It is the Chief Superintendent's grey Peugeot.

Mary runs up and, before he is able to get out of his car, she shouts: 'We've got it, boss!'

The Chief Superintendent smiles at her eagerness.

'Calm down Lester. It's not going to run away!'

Despite the smile, Mary feels her boss is tense. As they are walking along towards the shed, she glances at him sideways; his expression has taken on the harsh lines that both cops and truants often have in films. The bleak neon light from above further accentuates the sharpness of his face.

The drum is laying on its side, on the workshop floor.

Two trickles of water are running along the cement.

'So that's it,' says Fabien to himself.

He takes a couple of steps forward, bends over to inspects the drum, tries to move it and gets back up with a meaningful grimace. Too heavy. He looks at Mary who, seized up with anxiety, doesn't say a word. For a seemingly long time, silence reigns in the grease and petrol smelling shed.

A workbench has been built against one of the walls, with a vice on one end and a set of tidily arranged spanners hanging above it. The other wall is covered with shelves bearing chainsaws, drills and various pieces of equipment kept at the ready.

Is it the presence of the drum? Mary feels strange, a bit like in a church where speaking out loud would be incongruous.

At last the door opens and a middle-aged man enters the room, introduced to Mary as Captain

Laurent. He doesn't have Mary's scruples and speaks normally. He kicks the drum.

'So that's our surprise cracker then?'

'Yes,' answers Fabien. 'Can you open it?'

Captain Laurent examines the blue metal drum on which the brand of the oil it once contained remains in bold white letters: *Motul.*

'It shouldn't be a problem,' he says, getting back up, his examination completed.

And, to the tall blond who commanded the team on the river:

'François, bring us a hammer and chisel...' And, as François is leaving, he adds: 'Grab a sledgehammer as well, while you're at it.'

He turns to Fabien and Mary Lester to explain: 'First, we're going to cut the metal with the chisel, then we'll use the sledgehammer for the cement. It shouldn't be too difficult because it looks like fresh mortar and the sand doesn't seem to have been mixed in with the cement all that well.'

'On top of that,' adds Mary, 'he probably used sea water.'

'What makes you think that?' asks Laurent.

'If the job was done where I think it was, there was no other option.'

Perplexed, Captain Laurent glances at the superintendent. Fabien remains impassive.

So Captain Laurent shrugs his shoulders, as one who gives up trying to understand.

'Looks like a DIY fan, hey?'

'Some DIY fan,' echoes Mary.

She's not feeling that grand is our little Mary.

To tell you the truth, she wishes she were a few

hundred kilometres away. Oh God! What if she faints!... Well, she did ask for it... Fabien is gazing at her curiously, without saying anything. The tall blond has returned with the tools. He attacks the drum vigorously. His blows are deft and precise, the metal sheet splits easily. The blows resound lugubriously in this shed covered with fibrocement corrugated roof sheets.

Impassive, hands held loosely behind his back, Fabien quietly puffs on his cigarette holder. Mary is standing by him, arms folded and Captain Laurent is helping the fireman. The scene is dimly lit by a dusty lamp bulb hanging from the rafters.

The metal sheet has now been completely cut lengthwise. The firemen spread the two halves apart, careful not to cut themselves on the drum's jagged edges.

Water runs out, enlarging the puddle and a little crab —God only knows how it got into the drum— scuttles away to the first dark corner it can find.

'And there you are,' says Captain Laurent.

Now, they have to attack the block of cement.

'Pass me the sledgehammer, François.'

He slings one blow, then another and peers down to see the result.

The tall blond squeezes the chisel in the cement like a wedge.

'OK, leave it now,' says Laurent, 'I'll carry on with the sledgehammer.'

He lifts the sledgehammer and lets it drop on the chisel with a vigorous "hrumpf". One blow is enough. The cement splits open like an overripe conker and delivers its noxious fruit. A sickening stench immediately poisons the atmosphere.

Dropping his sledgehammer, Captain Laurent steps back, his hand to his nose. Superintendent Fabien lowers his head, his entire face rigid, protecting himself behind a cloud of smoke. Mary Lester turns round and vomits.

Antoine Sallabert has just been recovered.

'Come Lester,' says the superintendent catching Mary's arm, 'this isn't a sight for young ladies.'

They take a few steps in the courtyard, thankfully breathing in great whiffs of delightfully fresh evening air. In the shed, Captain Laurent can be heard giving out his orders: 'François, get one of the men to help you disengage the stiff completely and stick him in a plastic wrapper. After that, straight to the morgue. And don't forget, this is serious, not a word to anyone.'

Then, he rejoins the two coppers.

'Well hey, some surprise cracker! Is it you who found this out, Mademoiselle?'

Mary nods and puts on a meek smile.

Fabien asks: 'Are they taking him straight to the morgue?'

'Yes,' says Captain Laurent, 'once they've wrapped him up…'

'Tell me Laurent,' asks Fabien, 'I'm sorry to insist but it's important for the rest of our inquiry, are you sure of your guys? I mean, discretion wise…?'

Laurent smiles.

'Don't you worry, superintendent, if anything leaks out, it won't come from here. Come on, let's go and have a well deserved drink in my office. We all need something strong after this.'

CHAPTER IX

'How's that cold of yours, Amedeo, better?'

'A little, Chief,' answers a sniffling Amedeo. 'Talk about rotten weather. You're down with the flu before you know it.'

'I asked you to come despite your illness because it seems all is not for the best between Mademoiselle Lester and yourself.'

Mary Lester is sitting on her chair, apparently mesmerized by the sight of her fingernails. Chief Superintendent Fabien, comfortably ensconced in his armchair behind his Minister-size imitation teak desk, is mechanically drumming his fingers on the olive green desk blotter. Opposite him, Amedeo and Mary Lester are looking daggers at each other.

Amedeo blows his nose, clears his throat and says:

'Mademoiselle Lester has a very fertile imagination and…'

'And Monsieur Amedeo has no imagination whatsoever,' interrupts Mary who has long learned that attack is the best form of defence.

'And a definite propensity to arrogance,' completes Amedeo glaring at Mary.

'Maybe it's my fault,' says Fabien wearily. 'Amedeo, despite your experience, you might not have the right qualities to oversee a trainee.'

Amedeo raises his hands in a gesture meaning: *Ah, well, if you start pulling out words like psychology, teaching skills and all those newfangled ideas, you're right boss, it's not my thing.*

Fabien continues: 'Well, Mademoiselle Lester, or trainee detective constable Lester should I say, is complaining that...'

Amedeo interrupts him: 'I know, chief... Mademoiselle is accusing me of entrusting her with an inquiry and then taking it away from her. It's true, I plead guilty on that one. However, given the way she was going about it and the line of inquiry she was following, I would have been guiltier still if I had let her continue. Mademoiselle Lester is made for writing novels, not for day-to-day police work.'

'You know, Amedeo, of course these newly qualified inspectors have a lot to learn from old-timers like you but don't forget that they're just out of police college where they've learnt all the new techniques that have been discovered in the past twenty years. What I'm saying is that you also might have something to learn from them.'

Once again, Amedeo gestures with his hand that he really doesn't give a monkey's what these young know-alls might have to teach him.

Mary Lester eyes him with disgust. He stares her out, as if saying: *You can always complain to whoever you want you little bitch, I couldn't care less. In two months, that old fart will retire and whoever takes over is going to rely on experienced detectives like me, not on bloody trainees.*

'Chief Superintendent,' says Mary looking at Fabien, 'yesterday, you told me a little story. Now, I'd like to tell you another. It's a wee bit long but you might find it interesting.'

She hears Amedeo pushing his chair back to get up and leave. Without turning her head, she says: 'I would like Monsieur Amedeo to listen to my story.'

Amedeo mimics exasperation but, as Chief Superintendent Fabien signals for him to sit down; he obeys, if reluctantly.

'On Monday16th of November,' starts Mary, looking straight ahead of her, 'around 5.30 pm, Monsieur Antoine Sallabert, manager of the Lanester CenterMarket, left home to go and chop some firewood in Kerhervy, or so he assured his wife. Now, if Antoine Sallabert did effectively go to Kerhervy, it was certainly not to chop firewood. He was due to meet a woman. Yes, this exemplary family man rented a small house overlooking the Blavet from widow Le Dantec and turned it into a rather cosy love nest…'

'What's this bullshit?' growls Amedeo, raising himself to leave.

'Please remain seated Amedeo' says Fabien dryly. 'Let Lester finish her story.'

Amedeo reluctantly sits back on the edge of his chair, grumbling. He ostentatiously crosses his legs and folds his hands over his knees. His face has *the things you have to bear in the police force these days!* written all over it.

'The husband of this lady, Monsieur Sallabert's mistress,' continues Mary, 'is suspicious as, and we shall come back to that point later, marital fidelity is not exactly the lady's cardinal virtue. So he follows her discreetly and watches her park her car by the water, next to a cream colour Renault Traffic van. Then she climbs up the pathway leading to the little house and enters. The door closes and the lovers are lost to the world. Outside, the cuckold mounts guard. And it's a long guard; one hour, two hours, maybe even three hours. At last, the door opens. The woman comes out, gets into her car and leaves. The cuckold hasn't budged. He'll sort the wife out at home when he gets back. But the other one, the lover, boy is he's going to understand the meaning of the word *suffering*!'

Amedeo is squirming on his chair, obviously itching to go. Apparently fascinated by Mary's tale, the chief super hushes him.

'Quiet! This is when it gets interesting.'

Mary continues:

'Antoine Sallabert is a man of order so he remains behind to tidy up. I know. I visited the house. It was impeccable: bed made, table wiped, carpet swept, crockery washed, dried, and put away. When he's finished his housecleaning, he leaves, trots down the path, gets his car key out and that's when the cuckold, all the more courageous that his very slim rival isn't even 1.60 metres tall, comes down on him like a ton of bricks. However, this is not the cuckold's lucky day for he ignores a rather essential fact: the little man is a third Dan judo black belt. He's even been a member of the French military team. So, before he knows it, the cuckold finds himself sitting on his bum three yards away. Now utterly enraged, he rushes back for another attack. Yet another none too gracious arabesque in the air and another sore landing. How many times does he get thrown? I don't know. All the same, he gets scared. He came here to give this jerk a good beating and it's him that being beaten up. Being a cuckold is painful enough, but a beaten-up cuckold is too much. He caries a gun. He draws it out and fires two shots. Judo is powerless against bullets. So now our cuckold is landed with a corpse. What's he going to do? In the good old days in Chicago, gangsters just chucked their conveniently weighted down victims into Lake Michigan. Our cuckold is going to do likewise. He remembers seeing a building site higher up the road. He drives the van there, loads an empty oil drum used by the workmen to collect rainwater to wet their mortar, grabs a couple of bags of quick setting cement and a spade. He returns to Kerhervy, shoves Antoine Sallabert's body in the drum and goes to the open-air theatre where he remembers seeing some sand. There, hidden by the theatre fence, he mixes his ingredients and fills up the drum with cement. After a couple of hours of work —he's not used to manual labour— the body is tidily wrapped up for eternity, or so he thinks.'

'Most thrilling,' croaks Amedeo. 'When I told you, chief, that she was gifted for making up stories.'

Now perfectly relaxed, Mary continues, ignoring Amedeo's interruption:

'However, our man still has a problem. What is he going to do with the funeral drum? Shove it in the water, here in Kerhervy? A bit hazardous. The place is too crowded in Summer. There's families who come here with kids who could try and break up the cement block. If only he could take it a bit further, out there behind the rotting trawler carcasses. But no way, the drum is much too heavy. However, he could drop it from the railway bridge. Our man is in luck. Because of the works in progress, there is no guardrail and the gangway is temporarily deserted.'

By now, Amedeo is dead silent. He is staring at Mary with a mixture of awe and hatred.

'It's midnight,' continues Mary, 'or maybe one am. There's quite a bit of fog around and a tenacious drizzle is falling. Not a soul around. Ideal weather for the job. He removes the barrier protecting the worksite, backs the CenterMarket van up the bridge access ramp and rolls the drum out. The quick setting cement has had time to dry. All that's left to do is roll the drum to the middle of the bridge and shove it in the water, right in the middle of the channel where the water's deepest, i.e. at the level of the second pier. But, as he's approaching the first pier, he hears footsteps on the metal gangway. Someone's coming! The cuckold panics and throws the improvised coffin overboard. Regrettable haste. It's only an honest tramp, Maurice Toussaint, on his way home from Lorient and *he* is certainly not going to walk extra kilometres just because of a stupid "no entry" sign. Now, a three-hundred-kilo drum falling in water from a height of twenty meters makes noise. So, of course when he hears the splash, he comes to investigate, thus signing his death sentence. The extraordinary thing is that, for once, Toussaint is not drunk. He has seen the cuckold and identified him for a man he well knows. So he trustingly approaches to ask what's the matter. The cuckold is in a quandary. The tramp is a talkative guy. By tomorrow, all Lanester will know that a very heavy object fell off the railway bridge that night and that Monsieur X (let's call him that for now) was on the railway bridge at precisely that very time. This is a risk our man can't afford. His reaction is immediate. A violent punch sends the unfortunate Winklestar to his ignominiously waterlogged destiny.

'End of witness. Now, he's got to return to Kerhervy for his own car. But he doesn't want the van to be found here. There are always a few cars parked on the Restaurant du Bonhomme car park so he leaves it there with the keys dangling from the dashboard, hoping it'll be stolen and driven as far away as possible, which should confuse the issue nicely.

And that is exactly what happens: a gang of youths steals the van. Inside it, they find the chainsaw. One of them then has a brainwave and suggests using it to enter a house. They attack the door of a country house but the neighbours, roused by the noise, call the police. The youths scatter and scarper, except for one, Francis Le

Gwen, who drives away in the van. Unfortunately, with the coppers in hot pursuit, he takes a bend too fast, crashes into in a wall and is arrested.'

'Chief, may I ask a question?' requests Amedeo in an exasperated tone.

'Of course, go ahead.'

Amedeo turns to Mary with a superior air.

'Were you witness to all this Lester or are you making it up as you go along?'

'Neither Monsieur Amedeo.'

'Oh, I see, you were visited by the Holy Ghost then were you?'

'No, Monsieur Amedeo,' answers Mary as serious as a pope, 'the Holy Ghost has nothing to do with it. I observed some facts and made my own conclusions. I deduced, if you prefer.'

'You deduced, did you? Ah well, you should tell us about that, it must be fascinating.'

'More so than you would think, Monsieur Amedeo. You see, when you saw me at the garage, I'd just spotted a circular mark on the floor of the van, most probably left by a heavy metal cylinder. This circle measured 0.58 m in diameter. Now, what is heavy, cylindrical and has a diameter of 0.58 m?'

'How would I know?' grumbles Amedeo.

'Of course you know. It's an oil drum, a metal oil drum like those found in any garage.'

'That's not the only thing that has a diameter of fifty eight centimetres,' blurts out Amedeo.

'Probably not,' says Mary. 'However, for the time being, it's the only one I know and if you'd care to name others, I'm quite prepared to consider other hypotheses.'

And, as Amadeo remains silent.

'Nothing comes to mind? Well I can't think of anything else either. So I'll stick with my oil drum theory if you don't mind. In the Kerhervy open-air theatre, I found a dribble of recently made cement...'

'So what,' says Amedeo, 'they've been doing masonry out there haven't they.'

'I said *recently made*,' says Mary. 'Now, the works you're talking about were done last spring. I discovered the same cement patches in the van and, just next to the open-air theatre, some tyre tracks deeply set in the mud. The tracks of a Renault Traffic van.'

'Why a Renault?' says Amedeo, 'why not a Peugeot or a Citroen?'

'Because, Monsieur Amedeo, the track width of the Renault Traffic is 1.52 metres whereas that of the Peugeot J5 is 1.65 metres, like that of the Citroen C35.'

'My, you're well documented; you sound like a car show dealer.'

'This information *was* given to me over the phone by a car dealer,' says Mary. 'These people are remarkably eager to give out information. I can even tell you that Mercedes vans have a 1.61 metre track width, Ford Transits 1.68 metre and Fiats...'

'That'll do Mademoiselle I-know-it-all!' says Amedeo. 'Now all you've got to do is give us the name of this mystery man.'

'Do you *really* want me to, Monsieur Amedeo?'

'Why not! Were already rolling in fantasy, let's see what else you're going to invent.'

'I've invented nothing. *You* are the criminal, Marc Amedeo!'

Dumbfounded, Amedeo stares at Mary and then at the Chief Superintendent.

'I beg your pardon! What exactly are you insinuating?'

'I am not insinuating, Monsieur Amedeo. I am well and truly accusing you. I, trainee detective constable Mary Lester, accuse you of the murders of Antoine Sallabert and Maurice Toussaint.'

Marc Amedeo blanches, and immediately puts on a great show of indignation. His hands are grasping the edge of his chair as if he was about to bounce up.

'You're going too far!' he shouts. 'Chief Superintendent... Boss.'

From his comfortable armchair, Fabien has been watching the entire scene through half-closed eyes, not unlike a large Tom cat. He raises his hand to appease Amedeo and says: 'Carry on, Lester.'

Mary continues.

'I started to find your behaviour suspect when you got so unjustifiably mad at me for visiting the Renault garage. I'd wasted precious police time? Fair enough, but you could have just given me a mild ticking off. It was of no consequence. Then I saw the blisters on your hands. Now, you're obviously not a DIY fanatic, I'd rather place you at the bookies than in a DIY store. To cut a long story short, you could easily have got these blisters from the shovel you used to mix the cement.

Then, I found a witness. Every Monday, around 6 pm. a van from the CenterMarket goes to Kerhervy, and this has been going on for at least a month. This van is always shortly followed by a Peugeot 205 convertible driven by a woman. Both vehicles usually go away some time around 8 pm. My witness believes, and rightfully so, that this is an illegitimate couple having a quiet bit on the side. Now, you'll object that this is November and that a roll in the hay, or should I say in the wet Autumn leaves, would really require considerable passion. It therefore seems reasonable to believe that this couple has a love nest somewhere. The only place in Kerhervy suitable for such activities is a large shed perched on the hill and overlooking the sea which belongs to widow Le Dantec. I discovered that this shed has been very discreetly rented by Monsieur Sallabert. Although he took great pains not to give his name when he did so, Madame Le Dantec formally recognised him on a photo I showed her. Between Madame Le Dantec's account and the van belonging to the CenterMarket, it is not unreasonable to deduce that this man was Antoine Sallabert. Any objections, Monsieur Amedeo?'

Amedeo raises his eyes to heaven.

'What a load of bull!'

Mary Lester doesn't respond and continues.

'Now remains the question of the woman in the convertible 205. I believe Madame Amedeo owns such a car, a white model. *You* are the cuckold, Amedeo, hammers in Mary.'

Amedeo stands up, a nasty grin on his face.

'Enough is enough young lady! I think you're going a bit too far there. Chief, I refuse to be insulted any further by this nasty little bitch. I request your permission to leave. I'm going straight to my lawyer and we'll see what action we'll take against this hotchpotch of lies, untruths and slander... My wife owns a white Peugeot 205 convertible? That's true, but she's not the only one in the area. Did your so-called witness note the registration of this car?'

'No, Monsieur Amedeo.'

'So?' asks Amedeo.

Then he turns towards Chief Superintendent Fabien, sneezes, blows his nose and says: 'And you allow her to continue?'

And Fabien, impassive: 'Please carry on, Lester.'

Amedeo shouts: 'This is outrageous!'

The more excited Amedeo becomes, the calmer is Mary.

'It's only yesterday that I became certain that you were involved.'

Amedeo's complexion takes on a greenish tinge. His eyes are like a hunted beast's and large drops of sweat are pearling on his brow. However, he puts up a fight.

'You became certain. How about a bit of solid evidence.'

'I'm getting there, Monsieur Amedeo. My drum's been the topic of the day in the entire station. Everybody had a good laugh. Everybody, except you. Things were getting a bit too hot. If ever I managed to get that drum fished out... This highly incriminating piece of evidence absolutely had to disappear. Now, yesterday's was a spring tide. That was handy. The ebb tide was sometime around 23.00 hours. All you needed was a boat and two oars. So you stole the *Angèle*, moored her to the drum at ebb tide and waited for the flow. Once the boat was afloat, it should have lifted the drum. Unfortunately, you'd picked the wrong boat. The *Angèle* was too small, or the drum too heavy, anyhow, both sank and you ended up in the water. You plodded your way back to the shore through the mud and caught a stinking cold in the process. It's then, when the chief told me you'd caught a cold, that I became certain of your guilt.'

Mary Lester is silent now. She's looking at Amedeo. He tries to keep his countenance but his face remains pale and tense.

'What do you have to say Amedeo?' asks the Chief Superintendent.

'I am amazed by the fertility of this young lady's imagination.'

'Yes' says the superintendent. 'That was my initial reaction as well.'

'You see!' shouts Amadeo triumphantly.

'Except that I changed my mind later, when we fished out the drum…'

'When you fished out…' says Amadeo in a strangled voice.

'Yes, when we fished the famous drum out and found the body of Antoine Sallabert in it…'

'The body of Antoine Sallabert,' croaks Amedeo, 'I didn't know…'

'No, you wouldn't, you were off sick. How could you know? But you were spared a rather nasty chore. The poor man was in a sad state. He had two bullets in his chest, two 7.65 millimetre bullets. Here they are.'

The superintendent playfully rolls two small metallic objects around on his desk between the tip of his fingers.

'You're in luck Amedeo, you're easily going to be able to wave aside Mademoiselle Lester's accusations. Ballistics will prove you right. If you'll please hand me your gun...'

Pale and sweaty, Amedeo remains petrified in his chair for a few instants. Then, he straightens himself and, pulling his automatic out of its holster, jumps up and grabs Mary Lester.

'Don't move chief,' he shouts, a crazed look in his eyes.

With one arm, he's got Mary by the neck and is pressing her against himself. With the other hand, he's aiming his automatic at Mary's right ear.

The superintendent instantly looses his usual cool, calm and collected composure. He springs up.

'Amedeo, you're mad! Drop that gun!'

Amedeo laughs and backs towards the door.

'But Amedeo,' says Fabien stepping forwards at the same time, 'what are you hoping for?'

'To get out of here,' growls Amedeo. 'I will never go to prison, Monsieur, it stinks too much in prison. Please Monsieur, don't even think of moving! I've killed the bastard who was screwing my wife. I killed the tramp. Another murder won't change anything, even if it does have to be a pretty young lady like Mademoiselle Lester, without whom nobody would have had an inkling. I'm going to leave this room, take my car and, if all goes well, you'll recover Mary alive. If all goes well mind you! You have no choice...'

'Lester, I beg you, don't try anything. Do whatever he wants. He's mad, completely mad,' says the bewildered superintendent.

Lester doesn't answer. In fact, Lester is scared stiff. She can feel Amedeo breathing down her neck and it's making her nauseous. Still holding her, Amedeo makes for the door and opens it with the same hand that is holding the gun. Mary Lester knows that it's now or never. In a flash, what's she learnt at police school comes back: kusushi, leg sweep and tsuri-komi-goshi. Before he realizes it, Amedeo is sent flying and finds himself flat out on the carpet. He's dropped his gun in the battle. The superintendent grabs it whilst Mary straightens herself, apparently unruffled by the exercise.

'Judo, Amedeo. Judo. Useful thing judo. That's the second time it's defeated you this week. Shall I handcuff him boss?'

The chief super looks a bit green around the gills. Impressed by Mary's demonstration, he nods his agreement. He switches the intercom on and his brief sentences immediately trigger a cavalcade in the corridor. Berger enters, closely followed by Le Moal. They stare at an ashen-faced handcuffed Amedeo.

'Oh, chief,' says Berger, 'what...'

The past few minutes have added years on Chief Superintendent Fabien.

'Inspector Amedeo has just admitted to the murder of Antoine Sallabert and Maurice Toussaint' he says wearily. 'Take him and register his statement. Go with them Lester. I'll see you later.'

CHAPTER X

Shattered, Marc Amedeo tells his story quite willingly, even giving details he hasn't been asked for and signs the statement laboriously typed by Le Moal submissively, without checking its content. Then, he slumps back in his chair and lights a cigarette, staring glassy-eyed into space.

Mary Lester reads the statement through.

'OK. It's all there.'

'Just as you had imagined,' says Berger with admiration. 'There's nothing missing is there?'

'There is,' says Mary. 'One thing is missing.'

'Ah? What?'

'The bullets.'

'The bullets? But I thought…'

'You thought we found the bullets in Sallabert's body? Me too. I was even counting on them to expose the bastard. Unfortunately, although the impacts were there, the bullet themselves weren't. Poor Sallabert was so skinny, Amedeo's bullets just went straight through him. There were no bullets in Antoine Sallabert's body.'

'And so?'

'And so, we pretended we had found them. Without the bullets, we had no evidence so I suggested to the boss that we just take two 7.65 millimetre bullets from any policeman's gun. Our friend here fell for it. If he had denied shooting, we couldn't prove a thing. In fact, we didn't have a leg to stand on.'

Amedeo smiles and looks at her.

'Well done, love'

Mary jumps up.

'For Christ's sakes Amedeo, will you please stop calling me "love"!'

Delighted with her reaction, Amedeo grins.

'And don't look at me like that' she shouts, mad. 'Le Moal, take the bugger to the nick before I do anything I might regret.'

The sergeant nods to Amedeo to move towards the door. He's embarrassed to jail a man who, only this morning, was his superior.

Amedeo follows him obediently, still grinning and looking ironically at Mary. Embarrassed, Berger seems lost in the contemplation of his feet. The door slams, footsteps are heard down the corridor; trainee detective constable Mary Lester turns round and, lost in thought, sits down behind the metal desk. This was her first investigation and she's thinking that her fate is decidedly not banal. First attempt, talk about a masterstroke: she sends her immediate superior to jail! Will she ever be able to do things like everybody else?

CHAPTER XI

Amedeo gone, Mary remains a while behind her desk, lost in thought. Berger, perched on the other desk is also pensive. His nails are drumming mechanically on the metal surface of the desk. He sighs deeply, as if regretfully leaving a dream.

'What now?'

Mary starts.

'What was that you were saying?'

'I said: *What now?*'

'What do you mean, what now?'

'Well, I don't know,' says Berger, 'what do we do now?'

Mary jumps up.

'I'll tell you what. I'll buy you a coffee, or rather, *you're* going to buy me a coffee.'

'That's a good idea' says Berger jumping up in turn. 'I'll buy you a coffee to celebrate your triumph.'

Mary stops dead in the doorway.

'No, you *owe* me a coffee —and an apology— for making fun of me because of that bloody drum. You're the bastard who went and spread the tale in the entire station. Go on, admit it!'

'I'll only speak in the presence of my lawyer,' says Berger laughing whilst mockingly placing his hand over his heart. 'You'll have to learn to forgive and let bygones be bygones you know, love.'

'Bastard,' says Mary giving him a mock punch which he evades.

The corridor is still empty.

'Well' says Berger, 'Amedeo's arrest doesn't seem to have created the kerfuffle I thought it would. This place is as dead as a doornail!'

He pushes the WC door.

'Wait for me a minute, will you?'

He's barely entered when Mary hears him crying out: 'Le Moal!'

Mary rushes into the cresol-reeking white tiled room. Berger is kneeling besides sergeant Le Moal who is lying on the floor.

'What on earth…?'

'Help me,' says Berger. 'Let's sit him up.'

The fat man is still only semi conscious. Once sat against the white wall, he can't even hold his head upright properly. Mary takes his hand and pats it.

'Hey, Le Moal, what's happened to you?'

'Look' says Berger pointing at the egg-shaped bump on the man's head.

'Wow! That's at least a pigeon's egg. I wonder what he did this with?'

'He didn't do it to himself, someone did it to him' says Berger gesturing towards the wooden bar that used to hold the rolled towelling. 'Guess who?'

'Jesus Christ!' says Mary scrambling to her feet, 'Amedeo! The bastard's run off. I did find him strangely docile when he followed Le Moal. You bet he was quiet, he was plotting his escape. We've got to warn the boss.'

She sprints down the corridor, knocks on the superintendent's door and walks straight in without waiting for an answer. Fabien is on the phone, visibly engaged in a tricky conversation with his hierarchy. He covers the receiver with his palm and says reproachfully:

'Well Lester…'

'Boss, Amedeo, he's done a runner!'

'WHAT!' shouts Fabien rising from his seat. His already pale face blanches. Then he remembers the phone and collects himself.

'Just a minute, *Monsieur le Préfet*, something new has turned up, an emergency… That's it, I'll call you back as soon as possible *Monsieur le Préfet*. Sorry about this…'

He hangs up. From blanched, his face is now rapidly turning an interesting shade of scarlet.

'What's that you said, Lester?'

'Amedeo, boss, he's escaped.'

'But how?'

'He'd confessed everything, boss, and signed his confession. Le Moal was taking him to the holding cells and then…'

'And then what?'

'Well, Berger and I have just found Le Moal knocked out in the loo.'

'But this is crazy' mumbles Fabien. 'Where's Berger?'

'In the loo, with Le Moal.'

The superintendent rushes down the corridor closely followed by Mary. Le Moal is still sitting where Mary left him and Berger is dabbing at his brow with a moist handkerchief. The sergeant seems to be recovering slightly but his gaze is still dazed.

'WHAT HAPPENED?' roars Fabien.

Le Moal closes his eyes and cringes as if the Super's voice was drilling a hole through his brain.

'From what I've understood boss' says Berger, 'Amedeo asked to go to the loo. Then he washed his hands and while Le Moal had his back turned, he disengaged the wooden bar holding the roll of towelling and whacked him one around the head.'

'Is that it Le Moal?' asks Fabien, still roaring.

Le Moal grimaces in pain again and closes his eyes.

'He's groggy,' says Berger, 'we ought to take him to the infirmary.'

'You do that,' says Fabien, walking out. 'I'm going to phone *Monsieur le Préfet.*'

Strangely enough, all is quiet in the station. Nobody seems to have noticed what has just taken place. Mary rushes downstairs to the reception desk. The sentry was having a quiet snooze and Mary catches him by the shoulder and shakes him unceremoniously.

'Have you seen Amedeo go by?'

The sentry gives it a thought.

'Amedeo? Err… No.'

'Are you sure?'

Once again, the sentry thinks back.

'Well... Yes... I mean, he hasn't gone by, at least not since this morning when he arrived. He must still be on the premises. What's the big rush?'

'Rush isn't really the right word, disaster would be more appropriate' says Mary turning her heels.

'What shall I tell him if I see him?' asks the sentry.

'That's not bloody likely!' grumbles Mary.

Amedeo must have used the back door that gives onto the yard where he parks his car. Mary pushes the little door and runs out on the tarmac car park. Amedeo's GS has gone. A guard is pacing in front of the gate.

'Have you seen Amedeo?' asks Mary.

'Yes, he just left,' says the guard.

'With his car?'

'Yes.'

'Which way did he go?'

The guard gestures vaguely. 'He went that way, towards the city centre.' Mary shrugs her shoulders. Fat lot of use that is! From the city centre, Amedeo can take any direction. The guard sports a magnificent blond handlebar moustache which he is smoothing gently whilst looking inquisitively at Mary.

Mary returns to the station and makes a bee-line for superintendent Fabien's office. He's on the phone again, laboriously explaining the situation to *Monsieur le Préfet*. He signals to Mary to enter, asking her with a nod if she has any news. She nods a "no" and Fabien shrugs his shoulders in resignation. At last, he hangs up after a last *but of course,*

Monsieur le Préfet, both weary and deferential.

Fabien's wrinkles have deepened in the past few hours and his eyes betray his tiredness. He buries his face in his hands and remains so for a short while, as if he didn't know what road to follow, and then, sighing, looks up at Mary.

'Now we're really in deep trouble!'

At last, he pulls himself together; he thumps the table with his fist, gets up and starts to pace the floor.

'Do you realise, Lester, that right now the Gendarmerie is setting up roadblocks to catch detective inspector Marc Amedeo.'

He stops pacing and, silent, stares into space. Then he resumes, in a monotonous tone: 'Detective inspector Marc Amedeo, suspected of two murders, escapes from the Lorient central police station! Oh boy! The papers are going to love this. I can just see the headlines. Two months before my retirement. Just my luck.'

'What can I do boss?' asks Mary.

'Nothing my dear' says Fabien sitting down again. 'You've done enough as it is.'

Surprised, Mary looks at the Chief Superintendent. What does he mean? Is this an allusion to her zeal, her commitment to discovering the truth? Maybe he thinks that if she'd just stuck to her statistics, as she'd been told, they wouldn't be in such a mess now. The tramp's death would have been deemed accidental, case closed, and Sallabert would be quietly macerating in the mud for eternity under the railway bridge. Once his name had been duly entered in the "wilful disappearances" file, day-to-day routine would have been resumed in Lanester and Lorient. Amedeo would still be the efficient detective inspector he'd always bcen and Fabien would be peacefully preparing his farewell speech. Right now, he would have been studying catering estimates for his farewell do and Mary Lester would still be filing complaints for broken windows and stolen rabbits in Lanester's tiny station, squeezed in between the bank and the vet's surgery. A nice and tidy little office; just like any other small business, in a way... But Mary Lester has sent all this flying. She hasn't respected the conventional scenario by which trainee detective constables just stick to filing complaints and do not get involved in anything else.

Fabien looks at Mary and says, in a slightly reproachful tone:

'Go on Lester, go home! What more do you want to do? The Gendarmes have been put on the case and the usual procedure has been activated... All that's left now is to face the journalists and give them the crusty details. And, believe you me, that's not going to be the most pleasant part of the programme.'

Regretfully, Mary leaves. She would have liked to be part of the hunt for Amedeo but, as the superintendent said, what could she do? So, she climbs into her Mini and drives home through the grey city streets.

*

The night seems never-ending. In between a toss and a turn, Mary's feels that her mind is stuck on *free-wheel.* Might as well put that energy to use. She tries to put herself in Amedeo's shoes. What would she do in his place? Everybody seems to agree that he'll probably head South and try to return to his native Corsica. If he makes it, he would then be very difficult to catch.

Somehow, Mary can't bring herself to believe in this theory. To her, Amedeo is the sort of man who's more likely to turn up wherever he's not expected. He knows all the tricks of the trade and isn't going to let himself be caught easily.

The next morning, Mary arrives early at the police station where the atmosphere is strange. People are whispering, like in a dead man's house. She has the impression that her colleagues are avoiding her, that she's not only being kept away from the investigation but also from any information which has undoubtedly turned up.

Her office, well, the one she used to share with Amedeo when she wasn't stranded in Lanester, is empty. No message. Berger's office is also empty and a policeman standing guard in front of Chief Superintendent Fabien's door informs her that the Chief is *in conference* and has given strict orders that he is not to be disturbed.

At a loss, Mary walks back down to the hallway and waits a while. The phone is ringing non stop and the on duty receptionist transferring the calls keeps glancing at her balefully.

She gets the disagreeable impression that she is not wanted here so she goes out to the car park with the intention of taking her car and going to the Lanester station. At least out there, no one is going to look at her with such hostility.

She's got the blues. She starts the car, and is just shifting into first gear when she sees Fabien and Berger run down the flight of steps and jump into a patrol car.

The white Renault pulls away like a racing car with screeching tyres. Mary's pulse starts racing. She hits the road. At the wheel, Berger, and he obviously means business. He has switched the gyro on and the two-tone siren is howling. The little Mini is having trouble keeping up and Mary's eyes are glued to the blue gyro.

The Renault takes the Lanester road...

*

The Pont du Bonhomme is a resolutely modern concrete affair spanning the Blavet in the direction of Quiberon as you are leaving Lanester. Just after the bridge, a *menhir*-shaped[Tr. Note] granite memorial planted in a tiny garden informs visitors that the bridge was built in 1974 and was inaugurated by a certain Monsieur Marcellin, Raymond to his intimates, who in his days was one of General de Gaulle's Ministers. Parallel to this structure, the remains of the old bridge are still visible although the roadway has disappeared: two tall dressed granite pillars harbour carved out

Tr. Note : *Wikipedia : A* menhir *is a large, single upright standing stone (monolith or megalith), of prehistoric European origin. The word menhir was adopted, via French, by 19th century archaeologists on the basis of words in the Breton language meaning "long stone" (compare Modern Welsh :* maen hir = *long stone).*

niches that used to house a statue each, *Bonhomme* and *Bonne femme*[Tr. Note].

One day, the petrified couple disappeared, stolen by unnamed individuals with a warped sense of humour. They were eventually recovered but, for fear of another kidnapping, they are now guarding the town hall. Despite their absence, the souvenir remains and the new concrete bridge is still known as the Pont du Bonhomme.

The superintendent's car is parked at the bridge entrance, next to the blue gendarmerie van and the red fire brigade van. On the bridge, an *Accident! Slow down!* sign is flashing.

Mary parks behind the white car. The guardrail has been torn out over a few metres. Cars are driving by slowly and the breach in the sturdy metal parapet triggers a variety of comments and mimics from the drivers.

Obviously, some car has jumped into eternity. Mary leans over, shivering. For the moment, there is nothing to see. Fifteen metres below, several metres of greenish water whipped into a whitish foam by a nasty north-easterly wind mask the vehicle.

With Berger still in tow, Chief superintendent Fabien walks towards Mary. He stops a few steps away.

'Ah, Lester! I should've known. A bridge with something under it… you were bound to turn up pretty sharply.'

'Who is it?' asks Mary, fiercely gripping the cold metal parapet.

'Haven't you guessed?' asks Fabien ironically. 'I've known you more perceptive.'

Tr. Note : *In French,* Bonhomme *and* Bonne femme *are popular terms for Man and Woman.*

'It's Amedeo!'

'See' says Fabien turning towards Berger, 'You can't keep anything from her. Come on then, you might as well join us now you're here.'

Down by the water, directly below the pier, two divers are getting ready.

They scramble down towards them. The slope is steep and their descent is made treacherous by the slippery rotting leaves and the brambles that ensnare them at every step. The superintendent swears as his hat gets whisked away by a low branch. Berger picks it up and hands it back to him. Fabien nods a thank you. He carefully dusts the grey *Fléchet*[Tr. Note] with his sleeve and cautiously continues his descent, minding his step so as not to end up on his bum which would have been fatal to both his dignity and his trousers. He isn't exactly thrilled either by the prospect of having to climb back up this sharp slope later.

A few boats are moored downstream from the bridge and the wind is whistling lugubriously around their metallic masts.

'So?' asks Fabien as he shakes hands with the two firemen who've remained on the shore.

The fireman nods towards the water. It's the tall blond guy who fished the drum out from under the railway bridge.

'They're at it. They had to come back for lamps, the water's so murky. But there is no doubt about it, the car is a metallic brown GS, registered under the number 1247 2B.'

'Registered in Bastia' notes Berger.

Although he'd been in Lorient for two years,

Tr. Note : Fléchet *is the brand name of a well-known French hatter.*

Amedeo hadn't bothered to update his car registration[Tr. Note].

'There's no one inside' says the fireman. 'The front and right side of the car are badly damaged.'

The second fireman chuckles and, jerking his thumb towards the bridge above them:

'Given the state of the parapet...'

The tall blond continues:

'The front left door is wide open...'

Lost in thought, Fabien stares at the green foamy waters gushing past him. Fascinated, nearly dizzy, he is absorbed in the contemplation of the silent mass driven by some invisible and irresistible power. One of Amedeo's favourite sayings had been *Don't cross your bridges before you come to them*. Fabien smiles at the irony of it. Amedeo had crossed this bridge alright, but in the wrong direction! His colleagues used to pull his leg about his "bridge" motto. *Yeees, we know Amedeo, "don't cross your bridges before you come to them"* was a frequently heard chorus in the station canteen... Poor Amedeo, why didn't he stop before crossing this bridge? It would have spared everybody a lot of trouble and saved his life.

Berger and Mary stand aside, silent.

A strange black rubber skinned creature emerges with a hiss, closely followed by another... The divers have had a hard job returning to the shore, palming vigorously against the current with their flippers.

'So?' asks Fabien.

The firemen remove their masks. Both nod negatively.

Tr. Note : *In France, number plates indicate the geographical area where the car owner comes from. For instance, a registration ending with 75 means the car is registered in Paris and 29 stands for the Finsitère area.*

'Nothing!' says one who then turns towards the tall blond: 'We're going to have to sling it, Louis.'

The second diver adds: 'Do you really think it's going to budge?'

'Not half it is!' replies the first diver. 'There's a really strong seaward current. It would be really stupid to loose the wreck. If we do, we'll never recover it, not in this…' To illustrate his point, he makes a broad arm-sweeping gesture which includes the Blavet's vast estuary, the open sea and the island of Groix, clearly visible in the distance. Both divers are sitting on the shore, mechanically playing with the water with their flippers. Fabien leans over.

'Nothing inside?'

Wiping his mask with the palm of his hand, the diver looks at him.

'Nothing, Monsieur, there's no one aboard. The body must have been carried away by the current. As I told you, the left side door is wide open. If the guy had fastened his seatbelt… But he obviously hadn't, so…'

He gestures vaguely towards the open sea, as if Amedeo was now navigating somewhere in the narrow channels between the islands of Groix and Belle-Ile.

Fabien takes a few steps on the red sandy shore, where strands of kelp mingle with dead leaves and pine needles to form a brown and black meandering tidemark. He breathes in deeply, taking in with delight this both sweet and pungent smell found only in these blessed areas where, twice a day, the sea flows up the rias to flirt with the waterside trees.

He turns around and, hands behind his back, strolls back to join Mary.

'Well, there you are Lester... We've reached the epilogue of this distressing affair. As the papers would say, Amedeo is now beyond the reach of the law.'

'Do you think that he...' asks Mary, not daring to finish her sentence.

Fabien isn't so shy of the word.

'That he committed suicide? Most probably. You see, Lester, despite what you may think, Amedeo was a good copper.' He looks at the young woman walking beside him. Doe's he guess the shadow of a dubious smile on her lips? Maybe. So, he quickly adds:

'Each one to his own style. There are several ways to go about the same job. You didn't like his methods, he didn't understand yours. However, one has to admit that he achieved excellent results. In the two years he spent working under me, Amedeo never failed. He solved all his cases and that's not so frequent.

'Precisely because he was an excellent policeman, he was well aware that our police force is pretty efficient and well knew that, sooner or later, most criminals are tracked down and handed over to the law.

'Now, Amedeo's was a crime of passion. Dozens of them are committed in France each year. Imagine that, after having killed Sallabert, he'd come to see me, handed in his gun and said: *Chief, I've killed a guy...* Naturally, he would have been arrested and tried but I bet you he'd only get a minimal sentence. A suspended sentence… He's a cuckold, he's attacked by his wife's lover, he shoots to defend himself. Even the worst court appointed lawyer would draw tears from the jury with this.'

'Except that' says Mary, 'except that he'd be kicked out of the police force.'

Fabien sighs.

'You're right, Lester, he'd be kicked out of the police. And that's what pushed him to chose this way out. He was going to loose the job he loves, he was going to be punished when it wasn't his fault… Because that's what he thought, you know. In his mind, it wasn't his fault. Never forget injustice, Lester! Injustice is one of the most potent and widespread motives. Take these youths for instance, those who nick the mopeds and leather jackets of their more fortunate pals. They're young and life hasn't dealt them the same cards as others. Why? Not through any fault of theirs. So, in their eyes, this injustice fully justifies their behaviour. They deeply resent the unfairness of life and, as there aren't any more priests to preach resignation…'

The superintendent and Mary Lester scramble up the steep slope to the road. Breathless, Fabien stops half-way up and sits on a tree trunk felled by the last storm. By now, he's too tired to worry about his smart grey trousers. He lights a cigarette.

'I won't offer you one, Lester, I believe you don't smoke.'

Mary nods negatively.

'No chief, I don't.'

'You're right,' says Fabien exhaling a puff of

white smoke with manifest delight… 'I'm winded now.' What he doesn't care to mention is that, on top of the tobacco, he is well in his sixties, has a generous paunch and suffers from a chronic lack of exercise.

Down by the river, the firemen are wading into the water again, equipped with a sturdy rope. They're going to moor the car, pending the arrival of a crane to lift it out of the water.

On the bridge, local authority employees are placing metal barriers in front of the gap and the gendarmes are dismantling their electronic display boards. Dense traffic has resumed in both directions with its assorted continuous rumble.

When the superintendent has got his breath back, they resume their climb, Mary swiftly, privilege of age, and Fabien puffing and panting. At last, they reach the road verge.

'Shall I drive you back chief?' offers Mary.

Fabien, looks at the tiny black Mini and smiles.

'Thank you very much Lester, but I've got my chauffeur.'

And he turns towards the Renault where Berger is waiting at the wheel.

CHAPTER XII

In Lorient, Mary parks her car on Place Jules Ferry, the nearest car park to the station, behind the exhibition centre. This concrete block sporting a row of multicoloured flags gives onto a little garden graced with a large mosaic ornamental pond where, on great occasions, a fountain is turned on. It certainly isn't as impressive as the fountain of Apollo in Versailles, but, well, it's the thought that counts, isn't it. Right now, the murky dried up fountain would be rather a depressing sight if it weren't for two dogs who are playing between its verdigris copper spouts.

In the background, a little old man is pensively contemplating the war memorial where two massive granite world-war-I soldiers, standing to attention for all eternity, are staring stony eyed at the *Sous-Préfecture* edifice.

The Lorient central police station, a long low grey building, stretches along the Quai de Rohan behind a row of iron railings. At the end of the street, the marina wet dock is full up, as indicated by the forest of masts sprouting from behind the leafless tree tops. Further on, facing the sea, the landing pier where, in summer, the ferry for the island of Groix regularly loads it's bellyful of tourists. Strange city, where it's easier to moor a boat in the city centre than park a car…

Mary pushes the heavy metal door and climbs up the stairs. Berger has reintegrated his office.

'Well, that's it then' says Berger on seeing Mary. 'Things have come the full circle…'

'What full circle?' says Mary gently whilst perching herself casually on the corner of his desk.

'What do you mean by *what circle*? But…'

'But what?'

'End of Amedeo, end of investigation.'

'True… if he's really dead.'

'What do you mean by *if he's dead'* says an indignant Berger. 'Do you really believe he could've survived such a fall?'

'If he fell, no.'

'What do you mean by *If he fell*?'

'Will you please stop repeating inanely *what do you mean*. Have you *seen* Amedeo's body?'

'No, but…'

'But what?'

'It's probably been carried away by the current!'

'That remains hypothetical.'

'Mary, you're too much!' cries out Berger, slamming his fist down on the desk. 'Come on, his car smashed the bridge parapet before diving into the water.'

'Yes'

'Did you see the height he fell from?'

'I saw.'

'He *has* to be dead Mary!'

'Yeees,' says Mary, unconvinced. 'He has to be dead, or he should be... However, I have not seen him. Neither has anyone else. And remember what Amedeo used to say himself: *You tell me Sallabert is dead, Lester, OK. But show me the body!* And Amedeo was right. It's only when we showed him Sallabert's body that he took us seriously. So, I repeat Berger, I will believe Amedeo is dead when I see his body, not before.'

Berger gets up and starts pacing the floor, shaking his head and hammering each point with his hand held together in front of him, as in prayer.

'Mary, you are really a pain! You *will* see the body. Some day, when a trawler brings it up at the Pont Coupé or in Kéroman.'

'OK. Give me a shout then and I'll really believe he's pushing up the daisies. Meanwhile...'

Berger drops down on his chair, whistling between his teeth.

'Talk about stubborn!'

This makes Mary smile. She asks: 'Tell me, what about the boss?'

Berger's face splits in a broad grin.

'Much relieved. He's been glued to the phone ever since he got back. The *Préfet*, the Ministry, believe me, the switchboard guy is working his fingers to the bone for a change. The boss even forgot to tell us off!'

'Fine' says Mary, 'I see everybody's busy. As for me, I'm bossless'.

'What do you mean *bossless*?'

'Well, you've just told me my boss was dead.

So, I'm off for a stroll.'

'Where to?' asks Berger, frowning.

'In town, here, there...' simpers Mary making for the door.

'Watch out kid,' says a suspicious Berger 'I wouldn't be surprised if you were heading for more trouble.'

'No, no. Not at all, you're imagining things. See you later, alligator!'

*

On the Quai de Rohan, cars are crawling along, bumper to bumper. Noon. Parents are collecting their kids from the Lycée Saint-Louis[Tr. Note]. At a street corner, in front of the Hôtel Mercure, a uniformed security man is pacing, walky-talky at the ready. It's the man with the magnificent blond moustache. He smiles at Mary and stops the traffic to let her cross.

She grabs a quick lunch in a snack-bar near the post office, and returns to her car. A strange story, that of Marc Amedeo. What could his wife be doing now? What could she be feeling? Pain? Pity? Relief? God only knows.

Mary returns to her car and mechanically aims for the Lanester log dock, where Aimable Maugracieux found Maurice Toussaint's body. She drives alongside the rows of black pickets emerging from the still waters and stops under the railway bridge. She gets out and walks along the river bank to the spot where the firemen landed the sinister drum. Late Maurice Toussaint's residence is still

Tr. Note : A lycée *is a secondary school in France.*

there. And will be for a while yet. The Germans' reputation for sturdy building is well-deserved. Another dropout will probably take Mo's succession shortly. For the time being, the place seems empty.

Mary stops in front of the large billboard planted there by the Marine authorities: *High voltage cables. Distance: 7 metres downstream from the bridge. No anchoring or mooring within 20 metres.* Isn't it this same board which triggered Amedeo's downfall? Probably. Fate moves in mysterious ways.

She climbs back in her car, drives through Lanester and ends up at the Pont du Bonhomme. It's as if she wanted to take in the place's atmosphere one last time, like someone just about to leave a familiar setting for good.

Having crossed the bridge, she turns around and stops a minute in front of the *menhir* bearing the inauguration commemorative plate.

A couple of steps bring her above the water. The metallic barriers temporarily blocking the breach in the parapet are the only remnants of last night's drama. She notes that there are no break marks on the road and that the kerb has been chipped by one of the car's tyre rims.

To her left, the Ocean, open waters. The high seas where, in the golden days of the East India Company, so many vessels set forth to find silk, ivory and spices...

To her right, the Blavet, sneaking inland towards Hennebont. This ancient City of ironwork, now rather lethargic, used to be a hive of maritime activity at the beginning of the Century. But the Blavet has now become a luxury yacht parking spot and a naval graveyard. Mary can see all the wrecks rotting away in the river curve.

Can one also see Madame Le Dantec's house from here? No. However, under the bridge, she spots a path following the coast to Kerhervy. Now, that's a handy shortcut. Only for pedestrians though.

She climbs back into her car and drives past the rubbish dump. The gipsies have left and a bulldozer is piling up huge mounds of earth to discourage other candidates from camping in this enchanting site. Whether they like it or not, the gipsies will have no other choice but to camp by the highway.

A steady drizzle has begun to fall. The air is strangely still and the weather mild: drizzling and mild, typical Brittany weather.

Mary switches her windscreen wipers on but they squeak for want of sufficient water so she turns them off again. She drives to the open-air theatre, as lugubrious as ever, and stops a while without killing the engine. Then, she drives slowly back to Madame Le Dantec's house. This is definitely looking increasingly like a pilgrimage…

Oh, yes, she must remember to return her key to Madame Le Dantec. Jiggling the key in her duffle-coat pocket, she gets out of her car. She wants to have a last look at the house before visiting the old lady. After that, finished. Once again, she climbs over the rustic wooden fence, inserts the key in the lock, opens the door and freezes, paralysed.

Like in the open-air theatre when she discovered the cement patch, a diffuse anxiety sends chills up her spine. Once again, she craves to turn and run towards the city's reassuring lights. But it's like her soles were made of lead, as if a superior will was nailing her to the floor.

From the depth of the room, she hears a creak and a wheeze. There's someone there! The atmosphere is stuffy, like some beast's den.

Another squeak. Mary would like to run down the path, scream, do something, anything. But she can't. She's petrified, paralysed in front of this unknown danger.

'Is that you Lester?'

A hand of ice grabs her heart. My God! That voice! That voice from beyond the grave. Mary feels her skin creeping, her legs turn to jelly and she grabs the door frame to steady herself. In the hut, it's pitch dark.

'Come on in,' croaks the voice.

Like a sleepwalker, Mary takes three faltering steps forward and puts her hand to her mouth to stifle a scream before groaning: 'Amedeo!'

'Don't be afraid, Lester.'

The voice is hoarse, but calm. From the depth of the bed, two fiery eyes are staring at her. An irresistible urge eggs her on. She takes another couple of steps.

'I knew that if someone was to find me, it would be you.'

His breathing is now muffled.

'You wouldn't have a cigarette by any chance?' and gives the answer himself: 'No, of course not. You don't smoke. That's what I've missed the most, Lester, the ciggies. I haven't eaten for two days but what I really miss are the cigarettes.'

A dreadful cough racks him. Now that her eyes are getting accustomed to the darkness, Mary sees him grab his side in obvious pain.

She stammers: 'Are you wounded?'

Keeping his hand pressed to his side, Amedeo catches his breath. 'Not much... Just a few broken ribs. It only hurts when I laugh, sneeze or cough. Thank God, my cold's finished. As for laughing, opportunities are few and far between these days.'

'What can I do?' asks Mary.

'Nothing, love. You've done plenty enough for me thank you.'

In front of this man she has hated so intensely and who is suffering, Mary suddenly feels terribly embarrassed, nearly guilty. 'Well, I had to...' she starts, suddenly feeling an urge to justify herself.

Amedeo grimaces and continues. 'Oh, yes, you had to. You're a true copper so you had to follow the trail to the end. Do you know what, love? You and I are two of a kind.' And, peering at her: 'I can't see you properly. You're against the light. You ought to close the door and light the candles. The matches are on the table.'

Mary complies and lights the eight candles on the copper candelabra. A yellow glow lights up the room and reveals a pitiful Amedeo, shivering with fever in the double bed. His bony face seems even thinner than usual and the flickering glimmer of the candles accentuates its bony structure. The rings under his eyes stretch down to the middle of his cheeks and his swarthy Mediterranean complexion has turned a nasty sallow colour. Add a two-day old beard… and you've got a perfect mugshot. All he needs is the ID card hanging from his neck with the black stencilled numbers… but that won't be long now.

Amedeo reads Mary's thoughts better than in a mirror.

'Not a pretty sight, hey?'

She shrugs her shoulders slightly, as if to say *So what.*

'Don't just stand there, why don't you grab a chair?'

Mary pulls out a straw seat chair from under the table and sits gingerly on it's edge.

Amedeo is observing her. The only sound is that of his laboured breathing. At last, he says: 'I shocked you, love, when I said we were alike, didn't I?' As Mary doesn't answer, he insists: 'Go on then, admit it, admit that I shocked you!'

'I don't see in what…' utters Mary timidly.

'No, you don't… Of course, I wasn't speaking of a physical resemblance. I'm an old man, you're young, you're beautiful… What I meant was that, like me, you've got a true copper's nose… If you hadn't been there, I would've pulled a fast one on them all. Fabien, Berger and all the others wouldn't have had a clue. Sallabert would now be quietly sinking into the mud under the railway bridge and would've disappeared completely after a few years. Winklestar would be resting in the communal grave and I, Amedeo, would still be a senior detective inspector… unrelentlessly requesting my transfer to Marseille, Toulon or Ajaccio. A transfer that I would have obtained in the long run. And I'd have gone back to enjoy the sunshine and wait for retirement. But'…

He lays back on his pillows and seems to drift off into a dream of deep rocky inlets, sunshine, pastis and carefree days. Mary remains speechless, sitting stiffly on her chair.

At last, he raises himself slightly.

'What's the weather like out there, love?'

'It's raining, the sky is grey and there's no wind.'

'I see,' says Amedeo, forcing a smile. 'A fine and penetrating drizzle that soaks you more thoroughly than a summer shower…'

'Yes Monsieur.'

'It's the drizzle, Lester. I've known droughts in Africa, tropical downpours that flood everything, carrying roads and people away… But nothing, nothing is more depressing than the drizzle in Lanester. Worse than hailstorms; worse than the *Mistral*… Do you know the *Mistral*, love?'

'Yes Monsieur.'

'And the *Tramontane*[Tr. Note]?'

'I've heard of it.'

Amedeo's Mediterranean accent has returned with the *Mistral* and the *Tramontane*. 'Well, I lost the *Tramontane* when I came here. Where I come from, when you say someone's lost the *Tramontane*, it means that he's lost his marbles, he's gone round the bend, in other words, that he's become crazy. You *have* to be crazy to ask to come to this Godforsaken country of drizzles and regrets.'

'Because it's you who asked to come to Lorient?'

Tr. Note : The Mistral *and the* Tramontane *are both cold strong winds that blow in the Mediterranean region and have the reputation of inducing madness in some people.*

'It's me' sighs Amedeo. 'Amazing isn't it? It's a long story…'

He stops talking to catch his breath and then continues, still wheezing and rattling.

'I've been both lucky and unlucky: lucky to do a job I loved, and unlucky in that I fell madly in love when I was over forty years old. This was love with a big L. I went head over heels for a twenty year old kid. Oh, love, she was as pretty as a Madona. I married her against the advice of all my friends. They were unanimous: *Watch it, Amedeo, you know how the saying goes…* but it was like water off a duck's back. I just thought they were jealous. I thought I was the cat's whiskers when I married her. But it didn't last.

'I'll tell you something I've never told anybody, because those words hurt: my wife is a whore. OK, a "call-girl" if you prefer. I know that's what the *de luxe* ones are called nowadays. Looks nicer. But all in all, they just remain plain whores. I later learned that mine was working for a Corsican pimp, a nasty piece of work, as dangerous as a rattlesnake. It's him who pushed me to marry her, hoping to cash in on me sooner or later.'

Once again, Amedeo stops speaking and only his laboured breathing breaks the silence.

This is totally surrealistic thinks Mary: the candle-lit hut lost in the middle of the woods with the old shady copper, delirious with fever, rattling on about his lost love…

Having more or less caught his breath, Amedeo continues.

'I told you I loved my job, I told you I loved my wife... What was I to do? Give up my job? Unimaginable! And to do what anyhow? What can an ex-copper do, if not become a crook... No way. Give up my wife? Unimaginable! I love her more than ever. If I loose her, I don't want to live any more. I thought I might find salvation in flight so I applied for a transfer, far away, somewhere up North, anywhere. And I landed in Lorient. But my wife didn't give up whoring for all that. Her pimp came all the way here to chase her up. I nabbed him and sent him inside... for a long time, too. It just so happened that cocaine was discovered in his luggage. Unlucky, wasn't it?'

He closes his eyes and smiles, savouring his reminiscence of the trick played on his rival. Then, looking at Mary again.

'You know, you really hurt me, love. Not when you arrested me. No. There, I rather admired you, as a copper. That trick with the bullets was really clever. It isn't Fabien, that asshole, who would have thought that up... No, where you really hurt me deeply is when you were rolling out your story and started talking of *the cuckold*. Without naming me, but definitely thinking of me, you were saying: *the cuckold did this, the cuckold did that...* That's when it really hurt.'

He's looking at Mary and she believes she can see a tear trickling down the side of his nose. Overwhelmed, she looks at the floor, feeling dreadfully guilty. However... however Amedeo has killed twice.

She looks up. Amedeo is staring at her intently

and says, as if reading her mind:

'I must tell you another thing, love. Your story made sense, oh yes; but you were wrong on one point.'

Surprised, Mary raises an eyebrow; Amedeo continues in a would-be persuasive muffled voice:

'I didn't kill Sallabert.'

This triggers a protesting gesture from Mary which doesn't go unnoticed by Amedeo. He raises his hand to arrest the objection she is about to voice but she still manages to say:

'But... you confessed!'

He shrugs his shoulders, and immediately winces with pain.

'I confessed, I confessed... Sure I did. What else could I do?'

He sighs.

'Listen love, I haven't got long to go...'

And, as she's about to speak, he raises his hand again to silence her.

'You'll tell me that a few broken ribs won't kill me. That's true. People don't normally die from broken ribs. But I've lost the taste for life. And there's no curing that.'

Mary, stiffly perched on her chair, is drinking in his words, fascinated. Amedeo wolves down some air with difficulty and says:

'You were right about when I jumped on Sallabert to teach him a lesson. It's true I was overconfident there... such a tiny guy. He caught me unawares... He did send me flying, but only once. I didn't get a chance to come back at him. I fell so heavily that I was knocked unconscious for a few minutes. My gun must have dropped out of my holster in the process. I vaguely felt a presence next to me before hearing two shots fired. I scrambled up with difficulty. Sallabert was lying on the ground. I didn't know he was dead yet. A car was doing a rushed U-turn on the reserve. Still dazed, I picked the gun up and fired haphazardly at the car through the bushes. Bad idea… Now, everything was against me. Sallabert had been shot with my gun. My fingerprints were on my gun, I was the cuckold… There was no way I was going to wriggle my way out of that one. Antoine Sallabert's body had to disappear.'

'But then' says Mary, enthralled, 'Who *did* kill Sallabert?'

'Hey, love, work on it a bit. It's not that difficult to guess.'

What comes to her mind is awesome:

'It isn't…'

She stops, scared by the enormity of what she's about to say. Amedeo encourages her: 'Carry on then. Its strictly between you and me anyhow.' As she remains silent, he goads her on: 'It's not so easy is it? Much more difficult to think a nice person guilty than someone you don't like. Go on then. Be brave.'

Mary lets out: 'Madame Sallabert!'

'Bingo! Right first time, love. Madame Sallabert. The grief-stricken widow who knew about her husband's escapades and caught him red-handed with my wife. Sallabert tailed my wife to Kerhervy, I tailed Sallabert and Madame Sallabert was tailing me. Talk about a procession. This was really the night of all tailings!

'Was she surprised to see me? I don't know. Anyhow, she remained in the background until I rushed Sallabert. She was probably eager to see him beaten up but, when she saw he was winning, she stepped in. My gun had fallen out of its holster during the fight. I was laid out flat and Sallabert was walking back to the van. Enraged, she grabbed the gun and called her husband. Sallabert was stupefied when he recognised his wife. She was certainly the last person he was expecting to see there. In fact, she *was* the last person he saw, period. As he was walking towards her, two bullets sent him to meet his maker. The murderess then dropped the gun and fled.

'That's when I regained consciousness, grabbed my gun, and... well, you know the rest. Bad move, I told you, but I was still dazed. A few days later, as could be expected, the widow came to report her missing husband. I bumped into her in the corridor, as she was leaving your office. That's when I twigged that she was the one who'd taken my gun and shot Sallabert.'

'But,' objects Mary 'how did you recognise her if you hadn't seen her?'

'She betrayed herself. You should've seen her face when she saw me! She thought I belonged to the Lorient station and wasn't expecting to find me in Lanester. On top of that, I recognised her perfume. You see, when I was lying dazed in Kerhervy, I couldn't see her but I could still smell and I come from Corsica where the *garrigue*[Tr. Note] is rife with fragrances so I'm very familiar with perfumes.'

Tr. Note : *The garrigue or maquis is a schrubland covering the central mountainous part of Corsica where evergreen schrubs such as sage, juniper, myrtle and wild thyme grow.*

'But why didn't you say anything to Fabien?'

Amedeo winces again as he shrugs his shoulders.

'There was nothing to tell, love. I didn't have a shred of evidence. There was no way anyone was going to believe me and I would have looked bad, the coward putting the blame on his victim. Believe me. I've been mulling over all this for days and days. I know widow Sallabert killed her husband. For the rest of the world, she's innocent and, no matter what, she'll remain so. And I absolutely forbid you to go and try to prove the opposite. The public image of the police force is bad enough as it is without feeding its detractors with incriminating arguments.'

Exhausted by his long monologue, Amedeo lies back. Then, staring at the ceiling, he continues in a neutral tone: 'For the tramp, it was me. Things roughly went as you said. But, if you hadn't been there, nobody would've found out. I suppose that anyhow,' he adds cynically, 'this would just have postponed the issue. My wife would have taken on another lover; no doubt about it. She's so beautiful! You don't know her, do you?'

No, nods Mary.

'She is very beautiful' says Amedeo whose face puts on an expression of infinite weariness. She's very beautiful, she's a whore, and I love her.'

He lies there, staring into space and Mary thinks he's dozed off. She gets up and opens the door. It's still drizzling. A pale moonlight is playing on the skeletons of the wrecks emerging from the dark waters. The area is deserted. What should she do? The poor man should certainly be taken to casualty pretty quickly… Yes, now that she has heard his unfortunate story, Mary pities Amedeo.

From the back of the room, a faint voice reaches her: 'Are you there, love?'

She returns to his bedside.

'I'm here, Monsieur.'

Amedeo sighs.

'Come nearer… Tell me, aren't you puzzled as to how I shoved my car into the Blavet? Because it's the first thing I would've wondered about if I'd been in charge of the case. What did Fabien say?'

'Fabien and all the others are convinced that you drowned and that your body drifted out to sea with the tide.'

A faint smile creeps up on his pained face.

'Fine. That was the most plausible explanation. However, what *did* happen is too fantastic for words. If anyone told me that story, I'd call him a liar. When I split from the police station after having knocked Le Moal out… By the way, how is our good Le Moal?'

'A bump' says Mary.

'Is that all?'

'One big bump and a good ear-bashing from Fabien.'

Amedeo seems relieved.

'Ah! Good. I didn't want to hurt him but he's such a hefty guy I had to strike him pretty hard to neutralise him. Once in my car, I drove straight ahead but soon realized my situation was pretty hopeless. The entire French police force was after me and I'd lost the two things I loved most in the world: my job and my wife. At first, I intended to go South, blend in with the locals, you know, and even maybe go to Corsica. It wasn't impossible…'

'That's what Berger thought you'd do.'

Amedeo sniggers.

'Because Berger's thinking now. That's news!'

Mary can't stop herself from smiling.

'Aren't you being a bit harsh?'

'Oh no I'm not. You know Berger. All he ever thinks about is gambling. He doesn't give a damn about anything else. When you told him about the drum…'

'He just laughed.'

'That's it, you see… he laughed. They all had a good laugh, and I laughed the loudest, both because I was pretending and because it suited me. In this station, like in any other, we all have our hobbyhorse: drugs, gambling, prostitution… but they're all trainspotters, the lot of them. None of them are interested by the next man's pet topic. However, it works out. All these fields of interest are cross-related and when you're a real copper, anything remotely suspicious catches your attention. Sorry, I'm getting carried away here. They can do whatever they want now anyhow, it's not my problem any more…

'Let's come back to the Pont du Bonhomme as that's where I hid, under the old bridge. I backed my car under one of the arches, no one could see me there. I waited for night to fall, mulling over the situation. Now, I said to myself, what if I do make it to Corsica. What am I going to do there? Take cover in the *maquis*? Live like an animal, hiding in a mountain hut and eating chestnuts? I'm a city guy. I need crowds, bars, noise, the smell of exhaust fumes... I would die of boredom in the *maquis*. So, in the end, I decided I preferred dying, period.

'I waited till the middle of the night for the traffic to subside. Then, I drove back up to the road, put the pedal to the metal and, in the middle of the bridge, turned the wheel sharp right. The shock was terrible, something bashed me in the ribs. Must've been the wheel... I sat there for a moment, stunned. I couldn't understand. I could feel the car moving but I wasn't in the water. So I opened the door and got out. And there... there... the car door was literally ripped out of my hands. A car drove by fast, briefly lighting up the scene. The parapet was ripped out over several metres but the car wasn't there any more! Boy, was I puzzled. I leaned against a bit of metal, clutching my ribs, faint with pain. I stood there a while, gazing at the abyss but didn't have the guts to jump. By an amazing set of circumstances, my car had been precariously balanced on the very edge of the bridge. The only thing preventing it from toppling over had been my own weight. When I got out of the car, the balance was broken and it toppled over into the water.'

'A right little miracle.'

Amedeo sniggers.

'If you want. Then I took the footpath to Kerhervy. I still had Antoine Sallabert's key on me. I'd searched him before cementing him up. Oh God Mary, that walk was pure agony! With each step, I felt as if someone was plunging a red hot iron into my chest. Never have I been so glad to find a bed.'

'But, what were your plans?'

'I didn't have any. I was at the end of my tether' says Amedeo in a broken voice. 'I knew the police were after me. I only crawled down there to get off the main road by sheer instinct. I walked at random and then I saw the hut... I wasn't exactly in a position to be choosy was I?'

The silence that follows is only broken by his laboured breathing although Mary does believe she can also hear him sobbing. Highly embarrassed, she walks towards him.

'Amedeo, I'm going to call the boss.'

Amedeo signals his disagreement with his hand.

She insists: 'I have to!' Then, in a gentler tone, she adds: 'You need treatment Amedeo...'

He groans: 'And a trial.'

'Yes, Amedeo, you will go to court. But its a *crime passionnel.*'

'The tramp wasn't.'

'No, of course not, but it stems from the first crime.'

'Maybe. And what about my number in the chief's office? And the assault on Le Moal?'

'That was between us, Monsieur. It needn't be mentioned.'

Amedeo sighs again. 'I'm afraid it does. But never mind, love. Your grand and I guess there's nothing else to do. You go and call Fabien.'

'Will you stay here?'

'I won't budge, I swear.'

And, as she eyes him suspiciously, he puts on a half-smile, half grin: 'Honest, love!'

So Mary gets up to leave.

'I won't be long.'

She closes the door and runs down the path. Jumping into her ill-treated Mini, she bombs off to Lanester.

*

The restaurant at the Pont du Bonhomme is still lit up. Mary stops on the big car park and goes into the bar.

'A coffee please, and a packet of *Boyard Maïs*. May I use your phone?'

The barmaid nods towards the phone booth and carries on wiping her glass. Mary rushes into the booth, inserts her coins into the slot and feverishly dials the station number.

'Hello. Is that the Lorient police station? Yes? Put me through to Fabien. Yes, that's it, Chief Superintendent Fabien. Who's speaking? Mary Lester, trainee detective constable Mary Lester. Please hurry up, its urgent!'

Champing at the bit, she follows the switchboard guy mentally and pictures him leisurely plugging and unplugging his leads . Oh, will you *please* hurry up!

At last, Fabien answers.

'Hello' says a disgruntled voice. 'Is that you Lester? *Now* what's the matter.'

'Chief, I've found Amedeo!'

'WHAT!' roars Fabien

Mary can just see him collapsing in his armchair with the shock. She repeats, stressing each word: 'I have found Amedeo.'

'But, that's impossible. Where?'

She toys with the idea of leading him on a bit but then, remembering the state she's left Amedeo in, she quits the guessing game and answers: 'In Kerhervy, in Madame le Dantec's house.' On the other end of the line, the Chief Superintendent is rattled.

'But... he's...'

'Alive? Yes, he's alive. In a sorry state but alive. Look boss, I've got to go back there. Come quickly and bring an ambulance.'

She leaves the phone booth, grabs the pack of cigarettes, chucks two ten-franc coins on the bar and makes for the door.

'Hey, you haven't touched your coffee.' says the barmaid.

'Drink it for me, will you? I'm hyped enough as it is.'

Used to seeing all sorts go by, the girl just shrugs her shoulders and retrieves the coins. As long as they pay her...

The tyres of the Mini screech as Mary pulls away and drives ruthlessly back to Kerhervy.

She runs up the path like the wind, opens the door and stops dead... The room is dark and the acrid smell of a still smoking freshly stubbed out candle snuff assails her.

'Monsieur... Monsieur Amedeo?' she says in a choked voice.

She feels a cylinder roll under her foot. She bends down to pick it up. A candle... She gropes her way to the table and finds the matches. She strikes one, lights the candle and goes to the bed. It's empty.

She swears: 'Shiiiit! He's buggered off again. Can't the man ever stay in the same place for more than five minutes at a time. He had promised... Oh God, will I ever stop running after him?'

She is speaking too loud, too quickly, a bit like children who start whistling to reassure themselves when they're scared in the dark.

As she backs away from the bed, something touches the back of her neck. She turns around in a jump, iced with fear, and screams.

Nobody will ever run after Amedeo any more. He is hanging from the main beam and it is his kicking legs that have knocked the candle over in his last spasms.

Shaken, Mary backs away to the door. The burning wax trickling on her fingers makes her drop the candle.

Far away, she hears the lugubrious wail of the ambulance and the two tone sirens of the police cars opening the way.

'Too late!' says Mary out loud.

She goes out, slowly closes the door and looks up to the pale moon, savouring the coolness of the drizzle on her burning face.

She's been doing far too much running lately, far too much. So, for a change, she walks down the footpath slowly.

The End

Lorient, October 1992.

About author Jean Failler

Jean Failler was born in Quimper where he has lived ever since. His childhood dreams were fed by the seafaring tales of his grandfather, a remarkable storyteller and professional fisherman who used to takes him aboard during the holidays.

For 20 years, Jean Failler worked as a fulltime fish-monger but, somehow, he still managed to write 16 plays (5 staged) and several short stories, children's books and historical novels. After selling his fish-monger's shop, Jean Failler was at last able to fully devote himself to his passion and has graced us with 29 Mary Lester investigations where good humour and intrigue are our travelling companions throughout Brittany, all with that special tangy flavour of sailor-borne irony.

About translator Anne Pietrasik

Born in London where she grew up until age 10, Anne Pietrasik now lives in Brittany and has been a freelance medical translator and interpreter since 1992. Her previous experience includes training and qualifying as a Registered General Nurse in Farnborough (Kent) and as a Psychomotor Therapist in Paris, nursing in French and English hospitals, translating 3 nursing books into French plus 3 years of full-time sailing in the Mediterranean, the Atlantic and the Caribbean and 7 years of singing on the streets of Paris.

If you enjoyed this Mary Lester investigation,
read #8 in the series,
already translated into English:

Mayhem in Saint-Malo (*La cité de Dogues*)

Translated from the French
by William Rodarmor

Mary Lester is sent to Saint Malo, the all time City of corsairs, to investigate the death of the young and beautiful wife of a local notability 8 months ago. For the local Chief Superintendent the case is non existent: death by natural causes, case closed.

Mary's instructions are to just spend a few pleasant days in Saint Malo, pretend to look up a few leads and corroborate the Chief Super's conclusions. But that's reckoning without Mary's insight and natural propensity for trouble! Follow Mary in this medieval fortress where dark forces are at work.

If you want to brush up your practical French whilst exploring Brittany and its mysterious and magic heritage, there are 28 other Mary Lester investigations written in simple everyday French:

http://www.palemon.fr

ÉDITIONS DU PALÉMON
ZA DE TROYALAC'H - N° 10
RUE ANDRÉ MICHELIN - 29170 ST-ÉVARZEC
DÉPÔT LÉGAL 2e TRIMESTRE 2007.
ISBN 13 : 978-2-907572-84-2
ACHEVÉ D'IMPRIMER SUR ROTO-PAGE
PAR L'IMPRIMERIE FLOCH À MAYENNE (68262)
Printed in France